Helen Bianchin

ALEXEI'S PASSIONATE REVENGE

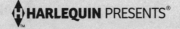

HARLEQUIN PRESENTS®

Recycling programs
for this product may
not exist in your area.

ISBN-13: 978-1-335-41900-2

Alexei's Passionate Revenge

First North American publication 2017

Printed in U.S.A.

www.Harlequin.com

ALEXEI'S PASSIONATE
REVENGE

For my daughter, Lucia, with all my love.

CHAPTER ONE

'GIVE ME A few minutes, then send her in.'

Alexei ended the call, slid the smartphone into the inside pocket of his jacket and stood in reflective silence as he studied the scene beyond the tinted plate-glass window.

Viewed from a high floor in an inner city office building, it appeared picture-postcard perfect with sparkling blue harbour waters against a backdrop of partially dark shrub-covered rock face showcasing glimpses of expensive real estate.

Sydney. The iconic Opera House, the expansive harbour bridge.

A large cosmopolitan city he'd departed beneath a deliberately fabricated cloud.

A city he'd vowed to return to in vastly different circumstances.

Which he had.

With a plan.

One which covered all the bases, and every possible contingency.

Five years ago he'd stood in this office space, denounced and discredited by Roman Montgomery, the owner of Montgomery Electronics, for daring to conduct a covert affair with Roman's daughter, Natalya.

A young woman who had enjoyed a life of wealth and privilege since birth. Intelligent, having graduated from university with an MBA degree with honours…savvy, and employed as her father's PA.

A life in which a thirty-year-old American *nobody* of Greek origin could never be a contender. As an added insult, Roman Montgomery had laughed at Alexei's expressed honourable intentions, written out a cheque in lieu of notice and issued an immediate dismissal, adding the rider Natalya had merely been amusing herself with a temporary fling. What followed became an orchestrated farce as Alexei's calls, emails and texts to Natalya were ignored, and within a matter of hours he discovered all her contact numbers had changed to an unlisted category.

Security guards posted in the main lobby of her apartment building ensured Alexei was denied access, and a determined attempt to reach her involving mild force resulted in a Restraining Order issued against him.

Which Alexei disregarded…to his folly.

The appearance of two police officers at his apartment with an arrest warrant provided a sobering experience at best. Invoking his right to legal representation ensured Alexei's incarceration was brief.

The desire to vent at what he perceived to be an injustice had been eased…*slightly*…by a harsh soul-destructive session with a punching bag at a local gym. He could still recall the cautionary shout from a fellow member nearby...*'Hey, man, you aiming to kill that thing?'*...resulting in one final vicious hit before he steadied the bag, tore off his boxing gloves, then turned and strode towards the changing rooms without so much as a word.

'Better a punching bag than Roman Montgomery's jaw,' he muttered beneath his breath as he stood beneath a hot shower to dispense the sweat from his body before switching the dial to cold in a bid to cool off physically, mentally and emotionally.

Within a matter of days Alexei had boarded a flight to New York, reconnected with his widowed mother, his two brothers in Washington and worked every waking hour, prepared to do anything within the bounds of the law—and a few that hovered on the fringes—in order to establish the foundation of an empire to rival others in the world of electronics.

And he had, exceeding his own expectations, aided by a new invention embraced worldwide that had elevated him to billionaire status.

During the past five years success and wealth had provided Alexei with much. Real estate in several countries, including a Paris apartment, a vineyard nestled on the slopes of northern Italy, an apartment in Washington, a Santorini villa inherited from his paternal grandfather.

Women? He'd bedded his share...a selected few of whom he continued to regard with affection. Yet not one of them had captured and held his heart.

While innate ruthlessness had ensured Alexei gained control of Montgomery Electronics, Roman

Montgomery's daughter fitted another category entirely.

Five years of planning, negotiating, dealing, had been with one goal in mind. To make Montgomery Electronics his own via the Australian arm of his global ADE Conglomerate.

No money had been spared in implementing state-of-the-art equipment at the electronics plant situated at one of Sydney's industrial sites, together with complete refurbishment of downtown city offices previously leased to Montgomery Electronics.

The media had featured the coup, speculated on the new owner's identity, and relayed Roman Montgomery's failing health, financial mismanagement and the global recession as the reason for sending Montgomery Electronics to the wall.

CVs and performance reports of existing employees had been examined, decisions made, with employment contracts prepared...currently in the process of being offered by Marc Adamson, Alexei's legal advisor, to selected employees for signature.

Among whom was Roman Montgomery's daughter, Natalya.

An act of vengeance?

Against Natalya's father? *Without doubt.*

Natalya?

The decision was personal.

Make that *very* personal.

CHAPTER TWO

THE MEETING WITH the new company's CEO was a mere formality, Natalya assured herself as she left Marc Adamson's office and made her way along a wide corridor with strategically placed alcoves featuring magnificent floral displays on glass-topped stands. Professional renovations, individual reception areas bearing luxe new carpeting, expensive leather seating, artwork gracing the walls.

A major upgrade from the old-school style her father had favoured.

A faint smile curved her generous mouth. New owner, new vibe.

From a personal perspective, there was a sense of satisfaction in having been offered the position as the new company owner's PA. The plus aspect being a very satisfactory salary package.

It would be interesting to discover how many office staff employed by her father had been retained.

As yet the new owner's identity hadn't been disclosed, with one media-projected rumour referring to an American-based billionaire.

If correct, she mentally sketched him as being over

fifty, maybe older, with access to inherited family money. Of average height, possibly bearing a paunch, together with thinning hair or a toupee.

A new broom sweeping clean…or perhaps a figure-head content to delegate and spend time schmoozing at various functions with the city's social elite?

Whatever…first impressions were key, and she tamped down the faint onset of nerves as she approached the CEO's executive area.

'We're not fully operational until Monday. Just knock on the door and walk right in,' Marc Adamson had instructed.

Okay, no problem.

She had a signed contract as proof the position was hers. All she had to do was smile, be professional and relax.

What could possibly go wrong?

Natalya curled fingers into her palm, rapped a firm double knock against the open heavily panelled door and entered a spacious office containing high quality furniture, floor-to-ceiling bookcases along one wall.

A quick glance revealed a wide custom-made desk bearing a laptop, various electronic devices, in front of which there were four single studded leather chairs spread out in a spacious semi-circle.

Within scant seconds it made a statement—wealth, excellent taste and power.

It was then she registered the tall broad-shouldered male frame silhouetted against a wall of reinforced plate-glass, affording an angled glimpse of strong features, a firm jawline, dark groomed hair.

A corporate wolf in his mid to late thirties clothed in black designer jeans, open-necked white shirt and a black soft leather jacket was vastly different from her preconceived image of the new company CEO.

A swift unbidden curl of sensation deep within surprised her, and was immediately discounted as a ridiculous flight of imagination.

Alexei held the advantage, one he used without compunction as he slowly turned to face the young woman who'd once shared a part of his life.

Dark almost black eyes regarded her steadily… waiting for the moment recognition hit.

As it did within a few fleeting seconds, and Alexei took pleasure in witnessing the faint widening of her eyes, the way her mouth parted, the quick swallow as if a sudden lump had risen in her throat as she visibly fought to school her expression into a polite mask.

Alexei? *Here?*

Coherent words momentarily failed her big-time, as she struggled to control the feeling she'd been hit by a forceful, if metaphorical, punch in the solar plexus.

Breathe, she bade herself silently as emotions rose to the surface, a gamut almost defying description, for how often had she attempted to cast aside images from their shared past?

Too many times to count.

Nights, on the edge of sleep, were the worst.

For it was then the memories returned to haunt her…the way his smile affected each and every pulse in her body; the gentle trail of his fingers down her cheek to trace her soft trembling lips. His mouth sa-vouring her own, teasing, tasting, as he drove her wild with wanting *more*. The heat in his dark gleaming eyes a prelude to mind-blowing intimacy.

Five years on there was no warmth apparent in his demeanour, just an inflexibility that sent a chill scud-ding down her spine.

What did you expect…a romantic reunion?

Seriously?

After five years… Are you insane?

From a time when she'd been able to accurately define his every expression, now she felt as if she'd been flung into a maelstrom of wild conjecture where nothing made any sense as he allowed the ensuing seconds to weigh heavily in the electrified air per-meating the room.

Her mind reeled with unvoiced questions. Initially, his motive to buy out the firm formerly owned by her father?

Rapidly followed by…how could Alexei Delan-dros have accumulated so much wealth in the space of five years?

Groomed designer stubble shadowed his jaw, add-ing an edgy quality, and there was a hardness ap-parent which didn't equate with the man she'd once known…and loved.

Natalya kept her eyes fixed on his in a determined effort not to escape his steady gaze. An act of de-fiance…or a mix of self-preservation and stubborn pride?

Both, she conceded.

Alexei took a degree of dispassionate interest as he examined Natalya's slender curves, narrow waist, slim hips, showcased in a black tailored business suit, with killer heels emphasising toned legs encased in sheer hose.

Subtle use of cosmetics enhanced her delicately boned face, emphasising expressive dark eyes and generously curved mouth.

The length of brunette hair styled into a sleek chignon made his fingers itch to free the pins to allow the thick waves to frame her face.

Professional cool...successfully achieved, Alexei admitted.

Absent was the vibrant, fun-loving girl who'd once embraced the world and all it had to offer. The sweet curve of her mouth parting in a laughing smile... eyes sparkling with teasing humour. The touch of her mouth on his own, magical, incredibly sensual as passion transcended to intimacy.

Alexei lifted one dark eyebrow in a gesture of musing cynicism. 'Nothing to say, Natalya?'

Where would you like me to begin? presented a tempting start.

Instead, she cut straight to the point. 'If this is some kind of sick game,' she offered with controlled calm, 'I refuse to be a part of it.'

He'd expected no less of her, given his deliberate act to conceal the new owner's identity from the media.

He inclined his head in silent mockery, enlightening, 'I prefer...a calculated strategy.'

Any sense of calm was discarded as anger rose to the surface, almost robbing her of speech as she fought the desire to slap his face hard.

'What else from a man such as you?'

Dark eyes speared her own. 'You have no knowledge of the man I've become.'

So very different from the Alexei she'd once known as memories flashed through her mind… hauntingly real for a few heart-stopping seconds as she recalled her body beneath his…supple, avid, in a manner that drove her wild.

For him, only him.

Dear God in heaven…*stop*.

Reflection in any form was a madness she could ill afford.

Almost as if he knew the passage of her thoughts he indicated the nest of chairs framing the front of his desk. 'Take a seat.'

Natalya spared him a dark glare, which had no effect whatsoever. 'I prefer to stand.'

He merely inclined his head…and waited.

An action which ramped her animosity up a notch, and her eyes speared his as she sought a measure of calm. 'The employment contract your henchman presented for my signature bears no mention of your name.'

'*Henchman*, Natalya?' The query held a vague musing quality. 'Marc Adamson is ADE's legal consultant.' He eased his lengthy frame against the edge of his desk as he spelled it out. '*Alexei Delandros Electronics.*'

'Very cleverly disguised in the contract I signed,' she accused as she reached into her satchel, removed the folded document, ripped it in half, then tossed the pages onto his desk, quietly pleased when a few of the torn pieces fluttered onto the carpet.

She wanted to hurt him, as she had been hurt by his abrupt disappearance from her life. Days when she could barely function. Nights where sleep eluded her until the early dawn hours.

Weeks, dammit, spent examining every possible reason he could have left without a word.

An inexplicable action which compounded when she woke one morning feeling queasy and had to make a mad dash into the en suite bathroom. Something she ate became less likely when a second early morning bathroom dash occurred the following day, and the next. A positive pregnancy test had tipped her into a state of shock…they'd always used protection, so *how?*…until she recalled a night when need had obliterated common sense.

A rapid calculation of pertinent dates had merely confirmed a distinct possibility, followed by a host of scattered emotions that briefly pitched her between delight and despair, and the inevitable…*this can't be happening*. Except a further three pregnancy tests over several days had eliminated any vestige of doubt.

Vivid images swirled unbidden through her mind of times shared, long nights together, the joy of love and quietly spoken plans for their future…then nothing, no word as to why Alexei had seemed to disappear like smoke in the wind.

The energy she expended attempting to track him down without success. Details of staff employed by Montgomery Electronics revealed Alexei's file had been deleted—but she had no idea who by or why.

It appeared he'd intentionally slipped off the radar...but for what possible reason?

She'd lain awake for nights searching for an answer...*any* answer. Only to come up with a few scenarios, none of which seemed to fit the man she thought she'd known so well.

Was she that desperate to locate the father of her unborn child, when he'd presumably taken steps to disappear? And what if she *did* manage to make contact? Would he be someone with whom she'd want to do battle over shared custody?

Seeking medical confirmation was a given, providing the reality of early pregnancy, closely followed by her determination to carry the child to full term. The only person in whom she'd confide was her mother...except she needed the right words, the chosen moment.

Only to have the decision taken out of her hands when she'd suffered a miscarriage just six weeks into the pregnancy.

A tiny foetus not meant to develop and take life's first breath.

There was little solace in medical opinion a second pregnancy would need to be carefully monitored with ongoing blood tests during the initial three months of pregnancy. Facts which didn't begin to equate with Natalya's emotional distress, until Ivana took action by booking flights and accommodation for a ten-day vacation on Queensland's Hamilton Island.

On reflection, they'd shared a lovely apartment with views over tropical waters, restaurants, time to relax and enjoy what the resort had to offer, indulging in facials, body massage, treatments at the Island's Resort Spa.

Sunshine, soft warm breezes, an idyllic beach. A healing period which strengthened their mother-daughter bond.

'Love you, darling,' Ivana had offered quietly as they exchanged hugs while the cab driver transferred Natalya's travel bag from the vehicle's boot. 'Are you sure you don't want me to come in with you?'

'I'm fine. Really,' Natalya assured her, aware once she settled into her apartment and resumed work as her father's PA life would assume its normal pattern... or as close to a facsimile of it.

And it had, over time.

All of which now flashed painfully through Natalya's mind, and served to heighten her anger as she rose to her feet, choosing to icily indicate the destroyed paperwork lying on the carpeted floor of Alexei's office.

'Not even a million-dollar salary would convince me to work for you.'

There was nothing she could gain from his expression, or his demeanour, then one eyebrow lifted to form a slight arch as he queried silkily,

'Are you done?'

Courage...she owned it in spades, Alexei acknowledged. Together with a flash of temper, which showed for a brief instant before she visibly gathered it in.

'Yes.' Succinct, and final.

Natalya turned to leave, and he waited until she reached the door before relaying with drawled intent, 'I strongly suggest you change your mind.'

He watched her shoulders stiffen, their slight lift as she took a calming breath before she swung back to face him.

With determined effort she took in his sculptured facial features accented by scrupulously groomed designer stubble…impossibly sexy, highlighting a raw edgy quality she found disturbing.

Dark eyes…not warm as she remembered, but cool, analytical. The faint groove bracketing each cheek seemed a little deeper, and the mouth which had caressed her own, devoured and taken, was now set in firm lines.

His shoulders…had they been so broad? His hair, so silky she'd exulted in ruffling it into disorder. Matching the dark promise in his eyes, a soft throaty chuckle an instant before he claimed her mouth, her heart…her soul.

Then.

Not now…and it rankled more than she would ever admit to how much the admission had the power to hurt.

She was over him. *Way* over.

Alexei Delandros belonged in a previous chapter of her life. One she had absolutely no intention of revisiting. Only a degree of stubborn pride ensured she remained facing him…when every cell in her body urged she should simply turn and leave. *So why didn't she?*

Because it was the easy way out. And she didn't do easy.

Like she'd even consider working for the man who had ruthlessly set out to destroy her father's business empire?

Natalya lifted her chin and threw him a fulminating glare. 'As far as I'm concerned, you can take your employment contract and shove it.'

She was either a very good actress, Alexei conceded, or she genuinely had no inkling of the verbal bombshell he was about to deliver.

'You might consider leaving your options open.'

Her eyes never left his own. Dignity and sarcasm didn't mesh, but she really didn't care. 'Please don't hesitate to enlighten me as to why?'

Family values had been her strong point. One he'd admired…until he'd dug deep into her father's business and private affairs and uncovered a number of discrepancies revealing the antithesis of the man Roman Montgomery managed to portray.

Had Natalya been aware of her father's transgressions? Possibly not, given Roman's penchant for subterfuge.

There was no point in sugar-coating the facts, nor did he feel inclined to soften his words.

'My accounting team have uncovered an elaborate scheme involving several bogus offshore accounts created by your father for the illegal transfer of Mont-gomery company funds.'

Alexei watched her eyes sharpen with disbelief. 'There's no way my father would commit fraud.'

It was a gut reaction and, on the surface, genuine, he perceived. Although she'd managed to fool him in the past.

'You're so sure of that?'

'I'd stake my life on it,' Natalya voiced emphati-cally, ignoring the folder Alexei extended towards her.

'I suggest you examine the paperwork.'

'And if I choose not to?'

He studied her features as she ran a pale lacquered nail over the folder's seam, noted the soft pink colour-ing of her cheeks, the defensive spark in the depths of her eyes, and for a brief moment he almost felt sorry for her.

Almost.

'The report details dates, account numbers, the series of complicated layers deliberately created to prevent detection.'

Natalya cast him a withering look, only to witness it had no effect whatsoever, and she tossed the report, unread, onto his desk.

'You can't be serious.'

The silence became an almost palpable entity as she refused to shift her gaze. Difficult, when a host of conflicting thoughts swirled through her mind.

If…and in her opinion it was a vastly improbable if…the report held a grain of accuracy, the question had to be what Alexei intended to do with it.

At best the details would reveal any fraud had occurred without her father's knowledge.

At worst...she wasn't prepared to give that thought any credibility.

'Read the report.'

Only a fool would fail to recognise the steely intent beneath his silky drawl, and she shot him a baleful glare as she picked up the proffered folder and flipped aside the covering page.

The first thing she noted was the name of the firm who'd compiled the data...and recognised it as one of the foremost sources well known worldwide for its excellent reputation.

Why did she have the instinctive feeling the goal posts had suddenly undergone a subtle shift, when it was she who'd determined to maintain control during this brief...*very* brief encounter?

A small ball of tension manifested itself in the region of her mid-section, and she took a calming breath before she began skimming the range of figures, dates, only to slow down as growing alarm escalated with each turn of the page. Detailed entries tracking each amount as it passed through an elaborate tracery of accounts.

A trail initiated by direct instructions from Roman Montgomery.

Amounting to millions of dollars.

Natalya felt as if she needed to sit down, and she froze for a few heart-stopping seconds as reality hit home.

If the report was brought to the notice of relevant

authorities, her father would face restitution, penalties incurred for tax evasion, and probable jail time.

It was beyond belief.

She lifted her head and looked at Alexei with undisguised incredulity for a few unguarded seconds, before reassembling her features into a taut mask as realisation hit.

'There's more.'

Natalya's eyes flashed dark fire as they fixed on his own. 'How can there be *more*?'

Alexei reached behind him, collected a second folder from his desk and handed it to her.

Her reluctance to examine the contents was apparent, and he watched in silence as her shoulders stiffened before she turned her attention to the written details, the photographs, and caught the moment irrefutable proof led to the only possible conclusion.

Roman Montgomery led a double life and had been doing so for many years.

There was an apartment in Paris, occupied by a mistress. A London apartment in fashionable Notting Hill housed a second mistress. Each of whom were maintained by Roman, whose visits coincided over the years with so-called business trips to both cities.

Deeds to both properties were buried beneath a list of subsidiary companies, ultimately tracing back to one man…her father.

Disbelief, together with emotions she was loath to name, coalesced into anger she fought hard to control.

The burning question had to be *why* had Alexei Delandros hired accredited investigators to delve deep into Roman Montgomery's business affairs and his personal life?

Why expend so much time, effort and money?

To do *what*?

Blackmail?

Her father? *Her?*

On the surface, such conjecture appeared unconscionable.

It took considerable effort to remain relatively calm, when her overwhelming desire was to toss both folders onto Alexei's desk and walk out, take the elevator down to basement car park level and exit with a squeal of tyre rubber.

Not the best idea…but incredibly satisfying. Provided she maintained control and didn't crash the car. Or worse, suffer an injury or three.

Her eyes darkened as they fused with his own.

'What do you intend to do with this information?'

Alexei regarded her thoughtfully, noted the tension evident in the way she stood, the straight back, squared shoulders, her eyes fixed intently on his own.

'That depends on you.'

The only visible indication apparent was a slight narrowing of her eyes, followed seconds later by an increased pulse-beat at the base of her throat.

A vivid reminder of past occasions when he'd touched his lips to that pulse, savoured it, before kissing it gently with his mouth. Her soft husky groan followed by a faint gasp as he used his teeth to tease and nibble a little.

Almost as if his body remembered, he felt its

damning response, and silently cursed as he shifted position, using the moment to transfer a slim document and pen from his desk and extend it towards her.

Natalya's eyes flashed with fine fury as she recognised it as a duplicate of the contract she'd just destroyed.

'I have no intention of attaching my signature to a document representing *any* company involving your name.'

'That's your final decision?'

'Yes.'

'You might care to consider the fallout if I disclose the information I have on your father to the relevant authorities and the media.'

He'd do that?

The answer was clearly apparent in the chilling darkness in his gaze, and her mind reeled at the impact the exposure would have on her parents, their lives, *her mother* once Roman's infidelity became known.

Anger burned her throat. 'You *bastard.*'

'Language,' Alexei chided mildly.

For a brief moment she wanted to cause him physical harm, unaware how well he was able to read her.

Silence filled the room…ominous, intrusive, threatening.

'Decision time, Natalya.'

The silky warning apparent in his voice acted as a reality check, and earned him a baleful glare.

'I need to consider my options.'

'There are two.' His gaze seared her own. 'You sign, or you don't.' He waited a beat, then added with irrefutable inflexibility, 'It's a simple no-brainer.'

Her father's indiscretions made public. Worse, much worse…her mother's humiliation and heartbreak.

The mere thought of the snide whispers, the disdain as the social elite tore her mother's marriage, her very life to shreds…

A silent curse rose and died in her throat. She couldn't do that to a caring, loving woman who in no way deserved such denigration.

Natalya subjected Alexei to a killing look which should have felled him on the spot, and gritted her teeth in sheer frustration when he displayed no reaction whatsoever.

'Give me the damn paperwork.'

Seconds later she tore it from his extended hand and began reading the various clauses. Carefully checking no word or phrase had been changed from the contract she'd initially signed.

Every detail was clearly defined, stating as his PA she'd be on call twenty-four-seven when necessary, and available to accompany him on business trips within Australia and overseas. The contract would be valid for one year…renewable by mutual agreement.

While a term of one year had seemed perfectly reasonable, *now* it stretched way too long. 'I insist renegotiating the one-year term down to three months.'

'No.'

His unequivocal refusal ramped up her anger to

boiling point. 'Revenge or blackmail?' she demanded tightly. 'Which?'

'Neither.'

He expected her to believe that? 'And the moon is a ball of blue cheese,' she offered with deliberate disparagement.

If he displayed so much as a glimmer of humour, she would hit him and be damned to the consequences. Only a forward flash of reality provided her saving grace, and she forced herself to mentally calm down, breathe, and stick to the basics.

'What guarantee do I have you won't go public?'

Alexei spared her a steely look. 'My word.'

'Not good enough,' Natalya dismissed with a re-taliatory edge, and glimpsed his eyes harden at her temerity.

'The original certified documentation is held in a bank's locked security box.'

She didn't hesitate in issuing a cool demand. 'Copies?'

'Returned to the bank's security holding after you've signed a new employment contract.'

'I'll require a certified bank receipt in confirmation.'

He leant back against the desk, seemingly relaxed, but only a fool would ignore the restrained power apparent, or doubt his intent to use it. 'Done.'

Her eyes silently warred with his own, her mouth tight as she fought for a semblance of control as Alexei handed her a pen.

A mesh of angry pride caused her to hesitate for a few seconds before taking it from him.

'Just for the record... I hate you.'

'An emotion which should make for an interesting relationship.' His voice was a smooth drawl which did little to improve her anger level.

'Business-related *only*.' The emphasis was fiercely stressed with finality as she attached her signature to a copy of the contract, watched as he countersigned, then she stoodto her feet, walked out of his office, and took the lift down to the basement car park.

Alexei was intent on playing hardball, expecting her to meekly comply?

Comply, yes.

There really wasn't an option.

But meekly?

Not a chance...

CHAPTER THREE

NATALYA ENTERED HER HOME, greeted Ollie, her beautiful Birman cat, caught him close for a customary cuddle, gave a light laugh at his plaintive miaow as she made her way into the kitchen.

'Okay, I get it. Dinner time.' She toed off her stilettos, dropped her bag onto the marble-topped servery, then moved to the walk-in pantry.

'Chicken or fish?'

Unable to answer, Ollie merely butted his head against her chin and began to purr.

'Chicken,' Natalya decided as she extracted the appropriate tin, removed the seal, spooned the contents into the cat dish and placed it on Ollie's food mat. 'There you go.'

Her apartment was one of two situated in a large two-level converted family home in an exclusive bayside suburb overlooking a sweeping promenade bordered by a stand of tall Norfolk pine trees along the seafront.

Inherited from her maternal grandmother three years ago, the home rested high on a sloping hill with sweeping views over the bay and neighbouring suburbs.

Renovated into two beautifully decorated apartments, one of which she leased to a responsible tenant, the property represented a valuable investment, providing Natalya with a place where there were no memories of her shared time with Alexei to haunt her.

Except now he was back.

Food held no interest whatsoever, and she reached for the remote, activated the TV, checked local and international newscast, and scrolled through the host of programmes until she found something that might provide a distraction.

A night in was a conscious choice. Not that she was a social butterfly, although there were a few very good friends whose company she enjoyed…live theatre, movies, social events for worthy charity causes; lingering over a shared coffee, and there was a sports complex she frequently visited with an indoor swimming pool, and several large rooms hosting a variety of exercise equipment. None of which held immediate appeal.

She wanted out of her clothes, a leisurely shower, then she'd slip into something comfortable and carefully examine her copy of the employment contract in the unlikely event she'd discover a possible loophole.

An hour later she tossed the contract aside, aware there appeared no evident room to manoeuvre within the skilfully crafted legalese.

Food was a requisite, and having nibbled without appetite she settled into a comfortable chair and channel-surfed the TV for a while, noticed a much-viewed programme, only to discover it was a repeat episode she'd already seen.

What next? Phone a friend? Skype? Flip through the pages of a current magazine?

Indecision wasn't one of her usual traits, so she decided to retire to bed with a good book. Ollie merely tilted his head in silent askance at this change in his mistress's usual evening routine, and leapt onto the bed when it became apparent Natalya intended to settle in comfort.

Half an hour in, the written word failed to capture her complete attention, given her mind seemed intent on reliving events of the day.

No matter how hard she tried to focus on the story, Alexei's image kept intruding, until she simply gave up, closed the bed lamp, and attempted to sleep…with no success whatsoever.

Emotional reflection eventually tipped her back into a place which transported her back six years to a time when she first met Alexei…at an end-of-year social gathering for employees of her father's affiliate firm responsible for the manufacture of electronic components.

Tall, dark-haired and ruggedly attractive, he'd stood apart from the rest of the men present. For a heart-stopping moment she'd become acutely aware of every breath she took, unable to look away as he turned slightly as if drawn by her attention.

Dark gleaming eyes met her own, lingered, before returning to the young woman who clung to his side. Understandable, Natalya conceded, given he possessed the wow factor in spades.

She could, if she was so inclined, cross to his side and effect an introduction. Hadn't she slowly circled the room achieving the social etiquette required of the boss's daughter separately, and at her mother's side, as the evening progressed?

Except she'd been forestalled by one of her father's foremen, intent on introducing his son, and when she moved on the object of her attention was nowhere in sight.

Shame, she mused, aware she'd probably never see him again.

Yet she did, days later, when she entered a suburban supermarket to purchase a few groceries needed to replenish her fridge and pantry. And there he was, in the same aisle. Their eyes met, and they both exchanged a smile at the coincidence, whereupon Alexei introduced himself, and Natalya did likewise. Coffee, the universal suggestion, worked, and led to conversation and the exchange of phone numbers.

What followed rose to the surface, intact and in glorious Technicolor…a relationship so special, caring, so attuned to each other there had been no need for words. Just the touch of his hand, the warmth of his smile, dear heaven, his mouth as it possessed her own. The hard strength of his body, aroused emotions taking them both to a place where they existed in a sensual world of their own. Erotic, exquisite, mind-blowing.

A time when she'd felt so happy…so *alive*, in mind,

body, and soul. Sure in her heart they were destined to share a life together.

Only to wake one morning to find herself alone in her flat, no explanatory note, only a brief text message on her cell phone later in the day indicating little, and not followed up at all.

'The number you are dialling has been disconnected', a disembodied robot had intoned, sending her reeling with alarm. Worse, the crushing news he no longer worked at her father's electronics plant.

Five years, with no satisfactory explanation.

For all she knew he'd disappeared off the face of the Earth, followed by months of her agonising *why*. Ultimately, the realisation he didn't want to be found.

Now he was back. Not the man she'd once known and imagined she'd loved, but a hard, resolute stranger bent on revenge—no holds barred. Bent on destroying her father, using her as a tool.

Blackmail…no other word suited as well.

She wanted to hit out…verbally, physically.

Silently didn't begin to cut it.

Getting physical, however, did.

First up, her apartment, which she cleaned to within a whisker of perfection.

A long session at the local squash centre expended excess energy, and there was a certain satisfaction in continuously slamming a ball against the wall, especially as she mentally imposed Alexei's body centre front and deliberately aimed to hit target every time.

Revenge of sorts for his physical image which had entered uninvited in dream form throughout the night, providing vivid memories she assured herself she'd long forgotten.

And knew she lied.

'Why so aggressive?'

Oh, hell.

Natalya closed her eyes, then opened them again as she turned towards her squash partner and endeavoured to catch her breath.

'There has to be a reason.'

Aaron offered her a penetrating look. 'Spill.'

One of the pitfalls of a good friendship being they knew each other too well.

Initially they'd met at a social gathering hosted by her father. A partner in a prominent law firm and the eldest son of a wealthy family, Aaron was sophisticated, charming and considered to be a very good catch in the matrimonial stakes. Only a chosen few knew he maintained a relationship with a long-term same-sex partner.

'Nothing I can't handle,' Natalya assured him as they emerged from the court.

Aaron read her better than most, a good friend who'd provided unstinting support when she'd needed it most.

Such as now, when his teasing anecdotes would do much to help lighten the dark mood threatening to destroy her composure.

'Share dinner with me this evening.' The invitation was tempting, yet she hesitated as she collected a towel from the neatly folded stack adjacent the locker rooms.

'I'll make a reservation and collect you at seven.' His smile held a tinge of humour. 'Enlighten me or not, your choice.'

She didn't, because she couldn't bear to drag into the open how deeply Alexei's presence affected her. Or revive memories too breathtakingly real to share.

Instead they kept the conversation light, touching on the ordinary, and simply enjoyed fine food, a little wine, and the relaxed benefit of good friendship.

It was a pleasant evening, and Natalya thanked him as he deposited her outside the entrance to her home.

Surprisingly she slept well and woke early, pulled on a Lycra body suit, added a singlet top, affixed earbuds to channel music and took her customary morning run…at a more gruelling pace than was her norm.

Following a shower, she dressed, munched on an apple as she collected keys, shouldered her bag and drove to the nearest mall to stock up on essentials.

As she drove to her parents' home later that day to share Sunday lunch she couldn't help but silently question what was *real*, as opposed to what had been a superbly acted sham on her father's part, given he'd managed to fool her so well. There were no incidents she could recall to indicate her parents' marriage had been anything other than a devoted union. There had been the odd private meeting while in London when her presence as his PA was not required. Likewise Paris.

The knowledge refreshed memories of her father taking time out for a relaxing massage. Personal shop-

ping time. The supposed private business meetings
he attended alone.

How naive had she been?

Worse, did her mother suspect?

Doubtful, given Roman had provided the perfect
cover by employing Natalya as his PA, ensuring his
daughter accompanied him to interstate and overseas
business meetings.

A string of silent castigations didn't come close to
easing the anger she felt at her father's deceit. There
was a part of her that wanted to confront him, rail
her fists against his chest and demand to know how
he could have put his marriage, dammit, his life, in
jeopardy by such selfish careless actions.

Play nice, Natalya cautioned as she eased her car
into the driveway leading to her parents' modern
home set in beautifully tended grounds.

Smile, chat, and pretend nothing has changed.

Except it had, and the conscious effort to maintain
a façade affected her appetite.

It was during dessert the question arose regarding
her future plans.

'Darling,' Ivana broached with interest. 'Are you
going to take a break before applying for another
position?'

Oh, my. Evade the issue, or aim for the partial truth?
It had to be the latter…

'No break, unfortunately,' she managed with a credible smile.

'Really?' Disappointment was apparent in her

mother's voice. 'I was hoping we might share some girl time. Lunch, shop. Book a massage, facial, mani-pedi.'

'Who will you be working for?' Roman queried, direct and to the point, as ever.

There was no easy way to break the news, other than to make the truth as simple as possible...then wait for the inevitable fallout.

Natalya met her father's narrowed gaze with outward calm. 'The ADE Conglomerate.'

His eyes hardened, so did the tone of his voice. 'You intend to work for the firm who bought me out?'

Natalya chose not to remind him that technically the bank had foreclosed.

'Is that a problem?'

Roman's features darkened. 'You're aware of the CEO's identity?'

'My interview was conducted by a legal representative.' Initially it had been, and not precisely an untruth.

The media presses would run overnight for newspapers delivered at dawn. In a matter of hours the news would become public knowledge.

'Alexei Delandros *is* ADE Conglomerate.'

'Delandros?' Roman's face grew dark with a mixture of anger and disbelief. *'Alexei* Delandros? What the hell are you *thinking*?'

Of my mother... Except the words never left her lips. Instead she lifted her chin a little and met his anger with determined spirit.

'He made an offer I couldn't refuse.' The truth... just not all of it.

Dark, almost black eyes hardened, and she saw his mouth thin to an ominous line as he made a visible attempt to rein in his wrath. 'How could you even *consider* working for Delandros?'

Because there's no alternative.

'In what position?' The demand was palpable.

With no easy way to break the news...except tell it as it was. 'PA.'

Roman regarded her with disbelief for several long seconds, then he slammed a fist onto the table, sending crockery rattling in protest. 'I'm calling my lawyer.'

'Who'll only confirm the contract was signed without duress and therefore legally valid.'

A telling silence reigned as Roman processed the inevitable. 'I hope you know what you're doing,' he warned heavily.

Her eyes didn't waver from his own for several seconds, then she discarded her dessert fork and pushed the plate aside. The thought of taking another bite of food made her feel slightly ill.

For as long as she could remember, she'd prided herself on being part of a close loving family worthy of her implicit trust.

Now she was forced to recognise the father she had adored was not the man she'd believed him to be, and the pain of betrayal was almost a physical ache.

The desire to leave was uppermost...now, before she uttered words that, once said, couldn't be retracted.

Another hour, that was all, then she could escape.

Consequently Natalya accepted coffee, lingered over it, and accepted Ivana's invitation to admire her treasured garden.

Together they moved outdoors, leaving Roman to add a generous snifter of brandy to his coffee, and smoke a cigar, presumably in the hope the alcohol and nicotine hit would soothe his temper.

Scrupulously tended and picture perfect no matter the season, the beautifully sculptured shrubbery and numerous borders were Ivana's pride and joy. While a part-time gardener took care of the heavy work, Ivana was very hands-on with the choice of plants and succulents designed to provide a glorious balance of symmetry and colour.

'Darling, I'm very concerned for you,' Ivana said quietly as they wandered through the grounds. 'Having to sell Montgomery Electronics was a blow to your father's pride and self-esteem,' Ivana added. 'It doesn't sit easily on his conscience he needs to rely on the money and investments I inherited from my late mother's estate.'

Natalya's grandmother had expressed a dislike of Roman Montgomery from the onset, and had been fiercely against the marriage, ensuring each and every one of her assets on Ivana's demise would pass directly to Natalya.

Natalya had adored her *babushka*, the regular visits with her mother, the joy and the laughter, tales relayed of an early childhood in another land, the treasures representative of a different country and culture…the division between wealth and poverty.

Ivana caught Natalya's hand and brought it to her lips. 'Will you find it difficult working with Alexei?'

The answer could only be an unspoken yes. 'I'm no longer the lovesick young girl of five years ago, *Mama*,' Natalya reminded her.

'Perhaps not. But...'

'I've moved on.'

You have? Like the initial encounter with Alexei Delandros was totally impartial and devoid of any emotion?

'I hope so,' Ivana opined evenly. 'For your sake.'

It was easy to offer a smile and brush lips to her mother's cheek. 'I'm fine.'

Little white lies and pretence. Not something she favoured, but forgivable in the circumstances... surely?

She lingered a while as they leisurely wandered through the structured pebbled paths, pausing to admire numerous plants, commenting on the subtle scent of roses, while listening to gardening tips Ivana chose to share.

There was a sense of relief when they reached the silver BMW parked in the pebbled forecourt.

'Come inside, darling, and have a refreshing drink.'

'Another time, *Mama*, if you don't mind.'

'You're leaving so soon?'

'New job,' she managed lightly. 'I need to check my wardrobe, laptop, and grab an early night.' She leant forward and hugged her mother close. 'Love you. Thanks for lunch.' A quick movement released the BMW's locking mechanism. 'I'll phone during the week.' She slid behind the wheel, fired the ignition, and blew a customary kiss as she eased the car forward.

Not the most convivial lunch, Natalya perceived wryly as she traversed the main road en route to her own home.

Tomorrow was likely to be a whole lot worse.

Working in close proximity to Alexei Delandros featured way down at the end of her choose-to-do list. So how did she prepare to meet her nemesis?

Perfectly groomed, elegantly attired, immaculate make-up, heels to die for…and presenting solicitous professionalism together with a degree of unruffled cool.

Something she achieved following two attempts to acquire the desired effect with her make-up.

Laptop, iPad, leather satchel, smartphone, car fob…*check*.

Minutes later Natalya joined early Monday morning traffic into the city, fought the long delays at numerous controlled intersections before entering the underground parking area assigned to the building housing ADE Conglomerate.

Easier said than done to tamp down the onset of nerves as she rode the lift to a high floor.

She'd been her father's PA for several years, she knew what the position entailed. There might be a few adjustments, but how difficult could it be?

CHAPTER FOUR

NATALYA ENTERED THE ADE reception and was met by a personable young woman who moved forward to offer a polite greeting.

'Natalya?' A hand was extended, which Natalya accepted.

'Marcie,' the blonde enlightened by introduction. The smile was genuine, which helped ease any pre-conceived tension. 'I'll take you through to your office suite.'

A comfortably large room, Natalya perceived, executive fittings, new state-of-the-art electronic equipment.

'Louise is your assistant, whose office is to your right, separated by a shared lounge,' Marcie offered with a smile. 'I'll introduce you, when we're finished with the tour.'

So far, so good.

'Alexei is at the industrial plant today. His office is to your left, accessed via his assistant's office, and their shared lounge.'

A reprieve, Natalya accorded, aware the day just became a little better.

Space, lots of it with room to move. Comfort,

synchronised professional privacy…and far different from her father's former set-up.

Introductions completed, Marcie indicated Natalya's office. 'I'll provide a brief overview of Alexei's schedule for the current week, and answer any questions you might care to raise before I leave to take a mid-evening flight back to the States.'

Efficient, capable and very clear re the CEO's schedule. One which Natalya reluctantly admitted appeared daunting.

Did the man sleep?

Not a wise thought, given it led to imagining if anyone shared his bed, and, if so, whom?

So what do you care?

You hate him, remember?

Focus, she admonished.

'I've printed out notes you may find helpful.' The attractive blonde bestowed a conciliatory smile. 'I'm confident you'll be fine.'

Natalya was sure she would be even if it killed her. For no way would she permit Alexei Delandros to have any reason to find fault with her performance.

As to her emotional heart…it was guarded in self-imposed lockdown. Deliberately sought, to regain a sense of purpose. Sure, she'd indulged in a social life, even flirted a little…if you counted a pleasant smile, intelligent conversation, light laughter.

Did anyone see beneath the façade? Detect her broken heart had been figuratively stitched together, never to be torn apart again? Healed, resolute, as she fought for contentment…and thought she'd achieved it, until a few days ago when Alexei Delandros reappeared on the scene and any pretence of contentment went out of the window.

Worse…unless she was wildly wrong, he'd deliberately taken advantage of her father's misdeeds to place her between a rock and a hard place.

Damn him.

He sought to play hardball?

Then so would she.

'Are you okay with that?'

Marcie's intrusion wrenched Natalya back into the here and now.

Schedule, overview. 'Got it.' At least she thought she had, and, failing that, there was Plan B… Marcie's printed notes.

Besides, she knew the electronics business well. Her father's list of contacts was on speed dial, and saved in her computer's email address file.

How difficult or different could it be?

Different, Natalya discovered soon after she entered the offices of Alexei Delandros Electronics the following morning.

Absent was the relaxed, almost laid-back atmosphere generated during her father's regime. Instead there was a fast-paced vibe as she passed through Reception. The receptionist's usual warm friendly smile was absent, replaced by a slightly harried look, and Natalya arched an eyebrow in silent query, only to receive an expressive eye-roll in return.

Alexei Delandros was in the building, and obviously bent on ensuring everyone followed a high-powered work ethic.

Which indicated she should merely offer a smile in return and walk on through to her office...instead she paused to indulge in a brief post-weekend chat.

Staff camaraderie had always been an important factor during Roman Montgomery's reign...

At that moment her smartphone buzzed and she retrieved and answered it, only to hear Alexei's secretary's voice.

'Natalya. Mr Delandros expects you in his office.'

Now...was an unspoken directive holding a slightly ominous tone.

'Two minutes,' she advised patiently, and fluttered her fingers at the receptionist before heading down the corridor.

A brief stop off in her office to deposit her bag and laptop, then she collected her iPad, breathed in deep and tapped on Alexei's door.

She could do this...and fervently wishing otherwise wasn't going to change a thing.

So ignore the man, smile, be so efficiently professional he'll have no cause for complaint.

Easy in theory...difficult in practice when all it took was a glance at Alexei's arresting features for her heartbeat to quicken. Worse, the sudden spear of sensation arrowing deep within her belly.

What was with that?

Her body out of sync with her brain. Granted, her polite smile didn't waver as she met his impenetrable expression.

The dark superbly tailored three-piece business suit, crisp dark blue shirt and perfectly knotted silk tie did little to tame the predator image.

If that was Alexei's aim…he'd unequivocally nailed it.

Cool, professional, remember? 'Good morning.'

One eyebrow lifted slightly. 'Your lateness is an oversight?'

Natalya checked her watch. Three minutes past eight. 'My usual start time is nine,' she managed civilly.

'I gather you failed to check your smartphone for messages…or your laptop?'

She had. Last night. Not this morning.

'Twenty-four-seven contact,' Alexei reminded her.

'Ultimatum,' she corrected without missing a beat, ignoring the silken warning apparent in his dark gaze.

He rested back a little in his chair and regarded her with a steady appraisal. If she was bent on a confrontational path…he was a few steps ahead of her.

'Written into your employment contract and specifically drawn to your attention during Friday's interview.'

Tough. While she had every intention of being the quintessential PA, and polite in the presence of others, any pretence when they were alone went out of the window.

She was something else, Alexei conceded as he took in her groomed appearance, the smooth chignon, skilfully applied make-up, red lipstick which matched the jacket she wore over a pencil-slim black skirt.

He experienced an urge to ruffle her composure, to dig beneath the professional façade. Then what? Rattle her cage?

His body stirred with sensual adrenalin, unwanted and inconceivable, but *there*. A *need* to pull her close and ravish her mouth…to remind her of what they'd once shared.

To what end? Play it forward to rumpled bed sheets and hot sex? Simply to satisfy an urge?

Evidence he unsettled her could be detected in the fast-beating pulse at the base of her throat, the edge of tension whenever he entered her personal space.

He had never aimed for the grab-and-conquer method with a woman. Mutual attraction and mutual need were his requisite for sex.

Natalya? Why this instinctive feeling there was a missing link? One only she could provide?

Patience. And time…the latter of which he had plenty.

Alexei indicated the structured curve of studded leather armchairs. 'Take a seat. I'll outline the day's schedule.'

Extensive, Natalya breathed as she noted appointments, calls to be made, two afternoon meetings to arrange…and lunch with a business associate.

'Book a table for one o'clock,' Alexei instructed, naming a restaurant with inner harbour views and known for its excellent cuisine. 'Contact Paul, my driver, and arrange to have my car waiting outside the main entrance at twelve forty-five.' His eyes didn't waver from her own. 'Naturally, you'll accompany me.'

Hadn't she attended many business lunches with her father? So why would this be any different? Professionalism ruled as she held his gaze. 'It would be helpful if you could reveal who'll be joining us.'

'Elle Johanssen and her PA.'

Natalya maintained a polite expression. Eleanor, or Elle as she insisted on being called, held a reputation for winning, by whatever means it took. Those among the business sector who'd parried with her and lost were known to refer to the woman as Hell-Jo... an unflattering but self-explanatory term.

Elle Johanssen, the noted ball-buster, locking heads with Alexei Delandros?

A woman associate with whom Roman Montgomery had refused to do business following one scalding episode that had left him red-faced and publicly humiliated.

Lunch should be *interesting*, to say the least.

She could do this, Natalya assured herself silently a few hours later as she rode the elevator with Alexei to the ground floor.

So why did she feel conscious of every breath she took, together with an incredibly heightened awareness that threatened to destroy her hard-won composure.

He radiated male sexuality, too much for any woman to ignore. Especially her, having known how it felt to be possessed by him. Sensual heaven...and then some.

Even now, when she had every reason to hate him, he still held the power to affect her emotions.

Five years…during which time she'd attempted to convince herself she was over him…disappeared like mist beneath rays of the sun.

Not good. Not good at all.

So much for self-survival skills.

And this was only day two in her contracted employ.

So…suck it up.

Which she did. Although there was a moment when Alexei indicated they share the rear seat of the chauffeur-driven limousine.

A deliberate ploy to unsettle her?

Who could tell?

She could analyse it to hell and back, and still not arrive at a definitive answer…so why even try?

The key being to adhere to the rules…a faultless PA during business hours, amenable and highly professional, even if it killed her, for no way would she allow him to glimpse so much as a chink in her emotional armour.

Consequently Natalya entered the restaurant at Alexei's side, where the maître d' offered a deferential greeting and led the way to their table.

Not the bar, which had been her father's preferred starting point. Or, she perceived in retrospect, where Roman plied his guests with alcohol before adjourning to a table where he ordered fine wine with no regard to cost. By which time, business, as such, became a secondary consideration.

Elle Johanssen made her entrance a fashionable five minutes late, offered a faux smile, apologised briefly as she slid into the seat politely held for her to grace it, and took control by ordering wine.

A female shark baring her teeth, Natalya mused, all too aware of the woman's reputation for shrewd deals tailored to her advantage.

In a contest of strong wills, Elle most often won out, her gritty formidability legend. So, too, was her intolerance for fools.

Natalya sat still, aware, alert…and prepared to watch the play between two business titans, each of whom were determined to win.

A little wine, which did nothing to soften Elle's forceful tactics…and the wheeling and dealing began.

It was quite something to watch, as Alexei simply listened while Elle outlined her terms, declared them non-negotiable…only to stiffen defensively as Alexei discounted all but one of them, before stating *his* terms.

Stalemate.

'You're new in town,' Elle dismissed haughtily, only for Alexei to qualify,

'But not new to business dealings.'

'My terms cannot be bettered.'

Alexei merely lifted an eyebrow. 'I disagree.'

'Really? By whom? A firm who'll use a superior to broker the deal, then pass the client on to a less experienced staff member?'

'No.'

Natalya saw Elle's eyes narrow in speculation. The ADE Conglomerate was huge. To have Alexei as a client would be a very large feather in the woman's cap.

It would be interesting to tell which card Elle would play.

'Then there is nothing more to say.'

Alexei's shoulders lifted in a negligible shrug. 'So it would seem.'

The word-play game had just moved up a notch.

A waiter delivered their entrees, which were eaten in supposedly companionable silence.

Was this the final act in negotiations, and, if not, who would concede?

Natalya's money was on Elle, given it was Alexei who held the power.

Conversation during the main course centred on world economics, a subject in which both Alexei and Elle were well-versed.

Dessert was declined, and Alexei chose not to linger over coffee, stating the meeting concluded.

That was it?

Unbelievable.

Alexei indicated Natalya take care of the bill with ADE's corporate card…which she did, following him from the restaurant to witness Alexei's limousine sliding to a smooth halt at the kerb.

It was then Elle moved a few steps to his side.

'Have your lawyer email me a copy of your terms.'

Alexei didn't miss a beat. 'There's no point.'

'I'm prepared to consider a few adjustments.'

Really? Natalya mused as she heeded the faint pressure of Alexei's hand at the back of her waist as Paul appeared and opened the limousine's rear door.

Alexei refrained from making any comment as

he followed Natalya into the rear seat and gave Paul instructions to leave.

'Checkmate?' Natalya offered with a tinge of cynicism, and incurred his measured glance.

Wednesday morning there was a courier delivery from Elle Johanssen containing an amended list of Alexei's terms. All of which, with the exception of three relatively minor clauses, Natalya noted, had been accepted.

'Return to sender,' Alexei instructed within minutes of perusing the document. 'With an attached letter rejecting the amendments, reaffirming ADE no longer require her services.'

Natalya keyed the relevant words into her iPad, glanced up and caught his slightly raised eyebrow.

'The three clauses are quite minor.'

Alexei's gaze was impossible to discern. 'I was unaware I requested your opinion.'

Was it her imagination, or did the room temperature suddenly drop a few degrees?

'You were present when Elle Johanssen requested a list of my terms,' he reminded. 'My parting statement to her was clear, was it not?'

'Perfectly. But she's…'

'Playing me.' His eyes seared her own. 'Something I refuse to allow anyone to do…under *any* circumstance,' he added in silky dismissal.

Okay, duly noted. Natalya collected the paperwork. 'I'll ensure this is returned today.'

'Via courier.'

Natalya inclined her head. 'Of course.'

'No further input you'd like to add?'

She didn't miss a beat. 'Nothing you'd want to hear.' Not the best exit line...yet there was a small degree of satisfaction in having had the last word.

And in doing so, she failed to see Alexei's lips quirk with mild amusement.

Natalya Montgomery was the antithesis of the carefree young woman he'd once known. Now she rarely smiled in his presence, which shouldn't concern him, yet it did, for he could too easily recall the way her voice would subside into a husky purr as he pleasured her. The sweet slide of her mouth when she caressed his body, teasing, tasting with such delicacy it drove him mad...until he took control, and it was she who gasped as he used his mouth to trace a tortuous path to the apex between her thighs, edging them gently apart to savour the acutely sensitive clitoris, using his tongue to drive her wild with need as she begged for his possession. And cried out as he moved over her and surged in deep as they both became swept up in the throes of a passion so intense there was only them...devoid of sense of time or place. So completely lost in an acutely sensual climax.

Alexei had contemplated for ever, his ring on her finger, a home, children...the complete package.

Only for everything to suddenly and inexplicably change.

Alexei leant back in his office chair and idly took in the cityscape, brilliantly clear on a mild summer morning. Beyond the many varied buildings the sky and sea appeared to meld as one.

The past couldn't be changed. There was only the present, and the future. Together with a plan…one he was determined to win.

CHAPTER FIVE

IT WASN'T SURPRISING the media channelled social and business reports around Alexei's every move…or so it appeared.

He was the new man in town. Successful mogul, ruggedly attractive with a dark earthy quality that had the social set flooding him with invitations.

Very few of which he chose to accept, preferring two prominent events, the proceeds of which aided worthy children's charities.

Both events drew national media attention, and resulted in photographic evidence of his presence with a different glamorous socialite clinging to his side. Each almost visibly simpering at having gained his notice.

Instructions for flowers…specifically roses…to be despatched to each socialite with the following message…

My personal appreciation for an enjoyable evening.

Really?
How personal was personal?

As if Natalya cared.

Although he did, in her eyes, redeem himself slightly by gifting a sizable donation to each nominated charity.

Laudable, Natalya conceded, or calculated…and mentally derided the latter as prejudicial, in spite of the fact he ranked *numero uno* on her list of least favourite people.

On the other hand she had to admit he worked long hours, for it soon became apparent he was the first to arrive each morning and the last to leave. No one could achieve what he managed on a nine-to-five schedule. A factor which had obviously enabled him to reach his current level of success.

His prominence in the business sector seemed to grow with each passing day, as did the respect of his peers.

Everything her father could…and should have had if he'd paid more attention to business instead of frittering company funds with magnanimous abandon.

Three weeks in, Natalya had managed to assume an admirable professionalism—no matter what Alexei threw at her.

And he did. Frequently, without warning.

If he was bent on testing her, she managed to rise to the occasion, and derived a certain satisfaction in holding her own…*professionally*.

Personally? Not so much.

As hard as she tried, she couldn't fault him. And she wanted to, badly.

Staff admired his business nous…especially the men. While the female staff sprang to sparkling attention every time Alexei appeared within sight.

Something Natalya chose to ignore, without much success. A fact which irked her unbearably.

She was over him. Had been for years.

So why did he enter her dreams and force a vivid reminder of what they'd once shared?

It was crazy.

This Alexei bore little resemblance to the man to whom she'd gifted her body…dammit, her soul.

Then he'd surrounded her with his warmth, his affection. *Love*, she amended, prepared to stake her life on it.

A time when she'd thought to hold the world in her arms, when nothing and no one could take it away.

Yet he had. And she hadn't been able to pick up the shattered pieces of her life.

The many nights she'd lain awake in tears searching helplessly for a reason *why*. Hoping, praying for a phone call, text, email…*any* form of contact that would provide an explanation.

Yet none had appeared, and slowly she'd managed to rebuild her life. Vowing she'd never let another man get close enough to melt her frozen heart.

There were friends, the trusted, tried and true kind, of whom Aaron was one. Ivana, her mother, another she'd trust with her life. Leisl, her BFF, who had married and now lived with her husband in Austria, with whom she kept in regular contact via social media, Anja, registered nurse and cosmetician to a leading Sydney dermatologist.

Acquaintances, of whom there were many, but not one of with whom she would lay bare her innermost thoughts.

The insistent ring of her smartphone dismissed any further reflection as she checked caller ID, picked up and briskly intoned, 'Natalya.'

'I'll require your presence this evening.'

Alexei issuing a statement, not a request. And there was no reason whatsoever for the faint shivery sensation feathering down her spine at the sound of his voice.

'I may have made other arrangements.' *May* ensured it wasn't exactly a fabrication. She even managed to sound suitably regretful.

'Cancel them.'

Just like that? 'If you'd given me more notice,' she began, only to have him cut her words short.

'Have you neglected to recall the terms of your salary package?'

Really? As if she could forget. 'Is it too much to expect a degree of courtesy?' Sweet she could do, albeit with a touch of saccharine.

For an instant she braced herself for his comment, only to feel slightly disappointed when he didn't rise to the bait.

'My car will be waiting outside your home at seven.'

Her chin tilted a little, a response ready…only to have him intercede before she managed so much as a word.

'Business, Natalya,' he relayed with an edge of mockery, and named a restaurant. 'Arrange a table for six between seven-thirty and eight.' Business… *naturally*. What else would it be? 'Of course.'

Selecting what to wear wouldn't be a problem, given her wardrobe included clothes suitable for every occasion.

Nevertheless she changed her mind a few times before settling for elegant evening trousers and camisole in deep jade, and teamed the outfit with black killer heels.

Understated make-up, emphasis on the eyes, a light gloss covering her lips, her hair loose framing her face, and she was done.

Her iPad was a given, satchel, smartphone, keys, a fine cashmere black wrap folded over one arm, and she was good to go with five minutes to spare.

Limousine and driver were waiting out front when Natalya checked, and she smiled as Paul crossed to open the rear passenger door.

'Thanks.'

She moved close, saw Alexei already seated, and bade a polite good evening as she slid in beside him.

The night was warm, the air-conditioning within the car set at a comfortable level, and she forced herself to relax as the limousine purred through suburban streets towards the city.

There was a moment caught up at a controlled traffic intersection when Natalya caught a glimpse of Alexei's profile outlined in sharp relief.

An attempt to be analytical failed miserably as she

skimmed those strong features. The firm jaw, broad
cheekbones, eyes as dark as slate, his mouth…

Don't go there.

Except it was impossible to still the sudden flare
of emotion in vivid recall of the way his mouth had
wrought havoc on every intimate inch of her body.
In the name of heaven…get a grip!

She did, in spite of the effort it cost her, and she
offered him a cool glance.

'Do you have anything to add relevant to this evening's meeting?'

All she had was a business dinner for six, time
and venue.

'No.'

Great. There was nothing like being unprepared…

'No comeback?'

She shot him a steady glance. 'No.'

For a brief second she thought she sensed a fleeting smile, then it was gone.

The car eased into a sweeping curve and slid to a
halt immediately adjacent the entry foyer of one of
Sydney's upmarket boutique hotels.

Alexei's associates were already seated as she entered the Bar Lounge at Alexei's side.

Four men of varying ages…three of whom she
knew by reputation. And Jason Tremayne, son of one
of the city's wealthy scions, who'd come on to her in
the past…charming in company, the reverse in private, as she'd discovered to her cost.

The tension racked up another notch.

'Natalya.' Jason's voice was almost as fake as his

smile. 'How *fortunate* you were able to score the position of ADE CEO's PA.' He waited a beat. 'But of course, you're old friends.'

The subtle emphasis didn't escape her, yet she managed a cool smile as she took a seat and ordered sparkling mineral water from an attentive waiter.

The evening's focus was business, and she assumed the expected role for which she was employed. A pleasant meal, during which her conversational input would be minimal. A few hours, then she'd return home.

Simple.

Except she hadn't factored in Jason's slightly raised eyebrow, the faint curl of his lip on occasion in a subtle reminder of a reckless mistake in judgment. Hers to have accepted his invitation almost four years ago at a time when she was most vulnerable.

Sydney's social elite were intensely active, organising and attending numerous charitable events for various reputable causes. A scene her parents had once been a part of for as long as Natalya could remember. Roman had considered Jason's late father as a business and social equal. There had even been talk at the time that a marriage between Natalya and Jason would prove a valuable business advantage. Something Natalya had refused to contemplate.

Until one evening, a few too many flutes of fine champagne, a starry night, and a determined need to move on with her life…the result had been a close encounter of the not wanted kind, ending with Jason's harsh words, a few hurtful bruises, and her desperate escape.

Something Jason had never let her forget, nor Roman's fall from grace in the business sector.

Alexei's reappearance in Sydney and his coup in acquiring Montgomery Electronics raised conjecture… So what if Alexei was flavour of the month and the rumour mill shifted up a gear?

Beating herself up about it wasn't going to change a thing.

'Indulging in a little mind-wandering, Natalya?'

Without pause she spared Jason a measured look and recounted a concise review of her condensed notes. 'I believe that covers it?'

She offered the three men a brief smile as the waiter appeared to request a preference for tea or coffee.

It was impossible to ignore Alexei's presence, or the effect it had on her emotions. A contradiction in terms given she had every reason to hate him…and she did. Unequivocally.

So why this simmering awareness? For no matter how strong her denial, her body possessed too many vivid memories to be easily dismissed.

Alexei Delandros was in her face…encroaching her space during working hours, and invading her dreams at night.

She was over him. At least she'd thought she was…until a few weeks ago when she entered the new CEO's office and discovered she'd walked into a living nightmare manipulated by a man she'd once loved so deeply, nothing, no one could possibly come between them.

So much for blind faith.

It was a relief when Alexei called time on the evening, and issued instructions to summon his driver.

'I'll take a cab,' she managed quietly.

'Not an option.'

Why, when the meeting was done and she was on her own time?

With the practicalities taken care of, Alexei's guests exchanged courteous pleasantries and made their way from the restaurant.

Natalya gathered her satchel. 'An emailed copy of my notations will be available on your laptop prior to the start of tomorrow's business day.' Professional efficiency delivered with firm politeness could hardly be ignored…surely?

Alexei pocketed his smartphone as he moved from the table and indicated the main exit. 'My limousine has just pulled into the kerb.'

'I've ordered a cab.'

He turned slightly and shot her a measured look. 'Cancel it.'

'No.'

If he brought up the twenty-four-seven thing again, she'd be strongly tempted to verbally lash out at him. It had been a long day, fraught with delays and interruptions beyond her control…throw in Jason Tremayne, and her composure was beginning to shred. More than anything she wanted the familiarity of her home and a blissful night's sleep.

'Do you particularly want to cause a scene?' His voice was a dangerously soft drawl, and she silently challenged him for several seconds, unwilling to capitulate.

The sight of a cab swooping to a halt directly behind the limousine proved perfect timing.

'There's my ride,' she indicated with polite civility, only to see Alexei cross to the cab, pay the driver, then return to the waiting limousine and indicate the open rear passenger door.

If a look could kill, he should have collapsed onto the pavement. As that didn't happen, she had to content herself with a flame-fuelled stare...one which, much to her mounting anger, he met with glittering dark eyes and held for what seemed a ridiculous length of time.

'Get in the car.' His voice was quiet. Yet only a fool would ignore the steel beneath the deceptive calm.

She tilted her head a little, for even in killer heels her height didn't come close to his own. 'You neglected to add please.'

Are you *crazy*? The answer had to be a definite yes.

He held the balance of power, and thwarting him to any degree was the height of folly.

For years, *hell*, most of her life, she'd complied, content to fit in. Happiness equated to family, good friends, satisfying job, and a pleasant lifestyle. Not that she didn't possess views, nor was she afraid to voice them when the occasion warranted it.

Easygoing, fun, joyful…until five years ago when everything had fallen apart.

Since then she'd toughened up…on the inside. Outwardly there appeared little change in her demeanour. As far as anyone knew, she'd survived and regained her former easygoing persona.

Only she knew it to be a protective shell. There were nights when vivid dreams haunted her sleep, occasionally so painful and stark she'd awake with tears dampening each cheek, emotionally and mentally exhausted by painful images.

'Natalya.'

Okay, enough with the hissy fit. One of them had to give in, and it was clear it wasn't going to be Alexei. Conceivably, how long could they remain standing here, Paul and the limousine waiting, in a deliberate face-off?

She gave Alexei a look that should have seared his soul.

'Go to hell.' The words were quietly spoken, but there was little doubt of the heartfelt meaning as she moved past him and slid into the rear seat, reached for the seatbelt, fastened it, and steadfastly ignored Alexei's presence as he joined her.

Silence is golden?

Really? It felt like a thick fog encompassed the car's interior as it moved quietly through the city streets.

She wanted to lash out at him in verbal rage…so much so it became a palpable entity.

'Nothing further you'd like to add?'

Natalya spared him a hard brief glance. The temptation to tell him precisely what she thought of his macho tactics was almost irresistible. 'Not at the present time.'

For a millisecond she imagined the gleam of humour in his dark eyes, and her own narrowed at the thought he might be amused.

She was tempted to take him up on it. Although the joke would be on her if it could have simply been a trick of reflected light in the car's dim interior.

Focussing her attention on the passing traffic, the bright neon billboards, worked for a few scant minutes, until unbidden memories rose to the surface.

Remembering too well vivid images of his mouth on her own. The way his tongue sought, teased in wicked exploration, and possessed until she became totally lost in the magic of his touch…and the response it evoked as she matched the sensual fervour to a point when foreplay ceased to be enough…

The images came to a sudden screeching halt as her mind went into involuntary shutdown.

She was so not going there.

Couldn't, if she was to retain a shred of sanity.

At least she managed to exert strict control during her waking hours…

Now he was there, five days out of every seven, invading her space, a constant reminder of what they'd once shared.

A deliberate manoeuvre in his plan for revenge.

Against her father…without question.

Her? How many times had she lain awake in the

dark of night emotionally agonising for a possible answer?

Too many times to count.

Alexei had done his homework too well, ensuring Natalya's one way out would involve irreparably breaking her mother's heart, and she hated him for it.

Worse, the all-consuming emotional war was gradually tearing her apart.

Had that also been part of his plan?

It said much for her resolve that she managed to regain a semblance of apparent calm until Paul turned off the main thoroughfare and eased to a halt outside her home.

Natalya unclipped her seatbelt, offered a polite goodnight, and made her exit, assuming a normal pace as she walked the path to the front door, inserted the key, entered the foyer, then closed the door behind her.

Inside the car, the driver spared his employer a questioning glance via the rear mirror. 'Seaforth, Alexei?'

He inclined his head, and issued a brief affirmative. Home was a beautiful mansion high on a promontory with enviable views. Professionally decorated and furnished, with staff to cater to his slightest whim.

Hard work, long hours, a penchant for electronic design…add the three Ds, determination, dedication and desire…had seen him succeed beyond his wildest dreams.

Some of his contemporaries had described him as

driven. Only *he* knew the true reason why he'd deliberately chosen to bring Roman Montgomery to his knees, and make Natalya pay.

There was a personal need to push the boundaries...which surprised him. So, too, did Natalya's concerted intention to become the quintessential PA.

Absent was her smile, replaced by an efficiency he couldn't fault.

Had she changed so much from the beautiful young woman in mind and spirit with whom he'd once fallen in love?

Haunting memories teased his sleep on occasion, and left him wondering if there was a missing link he'd failed to discover.

Yet he'd employed one of the best investigative teams to uncover fact, down to the most minuscule detail.

For a brief second he considered calling one of the few young women he'd dated socially, each one of whom had pressed a note with their smartphone number into his hand, issuing a sultry smile and breathing an inviting call me, any time.

Sex for the sake of it?

He'd taken his share. Indulged in short-term relationships that weren't destined to go anywhere.

Alexei checked his wristwatch, noted the time, aware the workforce on the other side of the world had begun, and there was data he needed to check, calls to make.

'Yes,' he conceded.

CHAPTER SIX

ALEXEI'S PREDICTION OF a full day fell short of the reality, as scheduled meetings ran late; an important presentation was held up due to an unforeseen delay, and there were occasions when the air in the conference room of an affiliate firm could have been cut with a knife.

The pace was relentless. A restless seemingly sleepless night meant Natalya needed to maintain focus, and as the afternoon wore on it took concentrated effort to keep up.

'Did you get that?'

Natalya met Alexei's studied gaze without so much as a blink. 'Of course.'

She did her work, executing each assignment with dedicated professionalism. No one was aware she downed painkillers for a persistent headache, or that her body became limp with relief when Alexei called an end to the afternoon meetings, issuing a curt demand to a contemporary associate to supply the relevant information within three hours or the deal was off.

Then he closed his laptop, gathered his briefcase, spared three associates a brief nod, and strode from the room with Natalya at his side.

Alexei's limousine was stationary in a temporary parking bay as they exited the building, and she slid into the rear seat, leaned back against the cushioned rest and appreciated the silence during the relatively brief ride while Alexei checked messages on his smartphone.

All too soon the limousine slid to a halt in the forecourt of their office block, where within minutes they reached the bank of elevators to take the first available one to their designated floor.

'Have Louise send in coffee, and arrange for food to be delivered here at six,' Alexei instructed, shooting her a glance as they approached his office. 'If you've made arrangements for tonight...cancel them. We'll be working late.'

'Tonight isn't convenient for me.' It was a retaliatory answer, despite being politely couched. More than anything she wanted to finish what was left of the working day, drive home, soak in a hot bath, then crawl into bed.

'Make it convenient.' Without a further word he moved to his desk and opened his laptop.

She was *so* tempted to utter a comeback, and almost did. Instead she turned away, effected an expressive eye-roll, stepped into her office and summoned Louise, who raised an eyebrow and offered, 'You look ready to slay dragons.'

For a few seconds she contemplated her weapon of

choice…not that it changed anything, but the image of winning provided momentary satisfaction.

'The CEO requests coffee asap.'

'Hot, black, strong. Got it. Anything else?'

'Dinner for two, to be delivered here at six p.m.'

Louise glanced up, pen poised over her iPad. 'Sourced from where? Preferences?'

Natalya named a nearby restaurant, specified orders, and waited until Louise retreated before allowing herself a faint smile.

Choosing Alexei's least favourite food would afford a slight victory of sorts…and if challenged, she had the perfect answer.

Meanwhile she compiled notes on an extensive report, and transferred it to Alexei's laptop.

Dedication was key, and it said much for her stoicism that she achieved an enviable workload. What was more, she managed cool…albeit polite cool.

By five-thirty most of the office staff had departed for the day, and promptly at six an alert came through announcing their dinner delivery.

Natalya checked the foyer camera onscreen, cleared the delivery, then went to Reception. Minutes later she collected two containers of food, paid the delivery guy, returned to her office and alerted Alexei.

'Take it through to the staff room. We'll eat there.'

Not if she could help it. 'I'll take a half-hour break at my desk.' Plus strong coffee and more painkillers.

Alexei spared her a brief glance as she deposited his food within reach, inclined his head in acknowledgment, and returned his attention to the screen.

Witnessing his reaction when he checked his meal would have been a plus. Although the visual aspect was less important than the deed itself.

The evening ran longer than anticipated, the pace full on…so much so, she began to suspect deliberate payback. Yet she refused to bend, achieving everything he threw at her until enough was enough.

With care she closed her laptop, stood to her feet and extracted her bag.

'You have a problem?' His voice was pure silk. 'We're not finished.'

Her gaze met his, fearless, unequivocal. 'I am.'

The air appeared to chill a little, and she stiffened her shoulders against the icy finger feathering down her spine.

'Angling for dismissal?' Alexei posed quietly as she stepped towards the door.

'Be my guest.' A foolhardy response, but right at that precise moment she didn't care.

'We both know that isn't going to happen.'

Natalya swung round to face him, and for an infinitesimal instant the atmosphere became electric. Her eyes met his in open defiance, silently daring him to react.

His eyes hardened, and a muscle bunched at the edge of his jaw. 'Think before you indulge in a war of words.'

'Really? *Why?*'

He waited a beat. 'Give it up, Natalya.'

'And if I don't?'

He didn't answer. There was no need.

She could plead exhaustion, a throbbing headache...she should probably apologise.

Instead she did neither, supremely conscious with every passing second of being alone with him in an empty suite of offices...no phones ringing, smartphones chirping or the buzz of background noise.

Were there others working in the building, putting in the hours? Who would know?

'Fifteen minutes should wrap it up for the night.'

Refuse or comply? The reality being comply... which she did, with a measure of reluctance. 'Fifteen. Not a minute more.'

Natalya caught his studied appraisal, met it briefly, checked her watch, then she returned to her office.

Precisely fifteen minutes later she shut down her laptop, pushed it into her satchel, gathered her bag, closed her office, stepped along the corridor...and found Alexei waiting in Reception.

'Thank you.'

It was an unexpected courtesy, and she found herself examining his tone for any hint of an edge, discovered none apparent, and merely inclined her head as she proceeded through the entry foyer to summon the elevator...which, despite a silent prayer, failed to appear within seconds, and left her little option but to share as Alexei appeared at her side.

Fate chose that precise second for the lift doors to open. Of course...what else?

Alexei stepped into the electronic cubicle and indicated the instrument panel. 'Which basement level?'

'Three.'

The small confines merely emphasised their isolation, and she hated his close proximity, the subtle aftershave which, unbidden and unwanted, succeeded in heightening her senses.

Nothing more than a temporary madness, she dismissed, more relieved than she was prepared to admit when the elevator slid to a halt.

The level was well lit and almost empty, given most of the building's staff had vacated hours ago.

With a brief goodnight, Natalya moved quickly towards her BMW, aware he remained at her side, and she pressed the remote button to deactivate the car's locking system, heard the resultant chirp and leant forward to open the door at the same time as Alexei did.

The touch of his hand on her own sent heat searing through her veins, and she quickly snatched her hand free, shaken by her reaction.

Worse, the unwanted flare of emotion deep within.

Get real. You have every reason to hate him, remember?

And she did, *really* she did.

So why was she temporarily locked into immobility?

Without a word she slid in behind the wheel, inclined her head in silent thanks as he closed her door, and she ignited the engine, eased the car out of the parking bay and resisted the desire to speed.

'Idiot,' she muttered beneath her breath, unsure whether the castigation was against Alexei or herself.

Both, she decided as she reached street level and joined the stream of traffic.

Ollie offered a plaintive miaow as Natalya unlocked the front door, and she scooped up his furry body, ran a gentle finger down his throat, sensed rather than heard his responsive purr, latched the door, then entered the kitchen, checked his dry food feeder and water bowl.

Stilettos off, briefcase deposited in her home office, then she headed through her bedroom to the adjoining en suite bathroom.

A leisurely shower, pyjamas, channel-surfing the TV, then hitting the bed were all on her agenda.

It had been a long day…not so much in hours, per se, but the pace. Achieving in one day what would have taken a minimum of several days during her father's regime, interrupted by over-long lunches, time out for one innocuous reason or another.

With hindsight it had been she who'd attempted to adopt a more businesslike attitude in preceding months leading towards the forced sale of Montgomery Electronics.

Takeover, she mentally corrected. Engineered by Alexei via an agent.

Payback. Undoubtedly justifiable revenge on Alexei's part…from his perspective.

How many nights had she lain awake wondering how their lives might have been if she'd been able to reach him when she first discovered her pregnancy?

Five years had passed, time during which she'd

carried on with her life, and managed just fine, she added silently…until Alexei reappeared on the scene.

Disturbing her peace of mind, her emotions.

In a deliberate ploy to unsettle her? Subtly remind her of what they'd once shared? The passion…the love.

A time when she could read him so well. The teasing gleam in his eyes, the curve of his mouth when he smiled. The barely disguised passion…a reminder of what they'd shared, and would again. *Soon.*

The light touch of his fingers as he trailed them down her cheek to cup her jaw, the slight pressure as his eyes darkened with passion…the light brush of his lips as they teased her own. The moment *teasing* became more…so much more there was no sense of time or place. Only pleasure of the senses, escalating until clothes became an unwanted restriction to be discarded at will…slowly, tortuously. Or almost torn with urgent hands until they each stood naked, exulting in the magic freedom of skin against skin and the mutual delight of touch to explore, tantalise and exult in mutual passion.

Natalya closed her eyes in a bid to dispense the memory, only to fail miserably.

Alexei's image was there, embedded in her mind, surfacing from a past for which there could be no return. Even now…especially now, there was a part of her that ached for what they had shared.

A past where she could read him so well, aware of the simplicity of curling her hand into his, the subtle trail of his fingers as they brushed her cheek.

Dear heaven, the quiet promise of how their day would end, the love they'd shared—so deep and all-consuming neither had any doubt it was the for ever kind.

Only for Alexei to suddenly disappear...and her world turned upside down, when hope died, together with the fact she needed to get on with her life.

During the past four years Natalya had studied advancement potential in existing technology—projecting how it could and would aid production. Increasing her knowledge in the field of electronics, creating ideas for media attention, publicity via donations to worthy charities...in each of which Roman showed little interest.

Her suggestion she join the directorial board had been dismissed out of hand. Reason being Roman was inured in the theory he had everything under control, and when he chose to retire, the lead role would justifiably be filled by a man.

Women, while delightful creatures, inevitably became tied up in relationships and/or marriage and children. Ergo, their attention became divided.

Natalya's rebuttal in naming women with high profiles worldwide who successfully managed both with admirable acclaim had been airily dismissed, followed by a reassuring pat on her shoulder and the words...together we make a good team. Why change?

Because if you don't, the firm will become vulnerable.

Words she had uttered at the time, to no effect whatsoever.

Never going to happen, Roman had assured her.

How wrong her father had been, Natalya reflected as weariness won and sleep provided a blissful escape.

Reflection served no purpose, Natalya decided as she guided the BMW through heavy traffic clogging main arterial roads leading from the city at another day's end.

A day fraught with action, demands which tested her ability to keep up with Alexei's instructions...so much so, tense didn't begin to cover it.

The man was a machine, geared into top form and take no prisoners mode. So chillingly calm, it sent figurative ice tricking down her spine...together with a degree of sympathy for whoever was his target.

If Alexei's motive had been an exercise in trialling the limits of her professional endurance...he'd positively nailed it.

There was the need for distraction, preferably something physical, where she could don boxing gloves and rid some excess anger against a punching ball...replacing the ball with a figurative image of him. There was a gym bag packed with clean gear in the boot of her car in readiness for a spontaneous workout should the mood take her...as it did now.

A flyer for a new women's only gym in a relatively new complex not far from her home had recently popped into her mailbox, and on the spur of the moment she decided to give it a trial.

Attractive signage, she acknowledged as she parked the car and retrieved her gym bag. Uncluttered reception area, boutique style with strategically placed mirrors, an attractive receptionist who took details, offered a friendly spiel, and alerted an attendant to escort Natalya on a explanatory tour of the premises.

Great state-of-the-art equipment, where a few participants played…the only word Natalya could think of, wearing the latest design in imported gym wear, full make-up, hair artfully tied back, at a pace aimed deliberately to avoid a sweat.

Seriously?

Her own dark grey sweat pants and matching sports top would stand out like a sore thumb.

Then she spotted a woman with a camera, and realised an infomercial was in progress.

'They're nearly done,' the attendant relayed quietly as she indicated a passage. 'The change rooms are accessed to the left. Each cubicle has an individual lock, a cabinet for your personal effects and an adjoining shower.' She handed over a key, offered a friendly smile. 'Enjoy your time here. Any questions, just ask.'

Feminine and functional…a pleasant combination, Natalya approved and she donned gym wear, executed a set of warm-up exercises before hitting the gym itself, initially setting a moderate pace before gradually increasing to near professional speed, maintaining it, then easing off. Taking time to hydrate, before moving on to a rowing machine.

Physical exercise, endorphins helped ease stress and tension…a clinical fact, Natalya acknowledged with gratitude as she took a leisurely shower more than an hour later, emerging refreshed, equilibrium somewhat restored by provided liquid lotions, clean casual clothes.

Natalya offered the receptionist a brief smile as she handed in the locker key.

'That was some workout,' the attractive blonde relayed with a degree of admiration. 'I hope you'll decide to take advantage of our membership.'

Maybe. The venue had high-end equipment, the facilities were fine, and it was close to home. There was no reason why she couldn't split her exercise regime between her regular gym and this one.

She was almost out of the door when her smartphone beeped with an incoming text, and she checked the screen, recognised the sender's number, and muttered something unprintable as she reached her car, aimed the remote, heard the resultant chirp, then slid in behind the wheel to check the message.

Current Passport USA Visa departure next week, destination NY. A.

Okay, she got it. Business, with scheduling details to follow.

CHAPTER SEVEN

THE REMAINDER OF the week progressed without a hitch as Natalya dealt with work, meetings, together with Alexei's seemingly incessant instructions. If, as she suspected, he sought to see her fall in a heap as he ramped up the pressure, she took satisfaction in being one step ahead of him by coping admirably... and then some.

The weekend loomed, with nothing planned other than her usual routine, and maybe a call to her close friend, Anja, suggesting they take in a movie currently gaining rave reviews.

Pleasant, low-key, enjoyable.

So why this sudden feeling of restlessness? As if there should be *more* to her life than a predictable pattern with little, if any variation.

She was happy with the status quo...wasn't she?

Because it's safe, a silent voice taunted.

A conscious choice, she determined. One with which she'd been perfectly content...until now.

The cause, she reluctantly admitted, was Alexei.

There. In her face. Invading her mind...her

sleep, as a reminder of what they'd once shared together.

Like she wanted to be caught up in an emotional maelstrom? Alternately dismissing the secret yearning deep in her heart, and the need to rail against him for causing it.

The electric fire of his touch when their hands met on the door clasp of her car in the bowels of the basement car park, when for one wild unprincipled moment she hadn't been able to *think*, let alone move.

Had he felt it, too?

For heaven's sake, take a reality check.

Alexei's sole motivation was revenge. Hadn't he gone to exceptional lengths to ensure he'd covered every possible angle?

So why waste time trying to search for that elusive something that didn't quite gel?

Worse, why was it *she* who was paying the price for her father's indiscretions and financial misdeeds?

Enough already.

Except her weekend plans were felled in one swift stroke with a text message received at ten fifty-three Saturday morning from Alexei demanding she contact him asap.

A soft imprecation escaped from her lips, followed by, 'Who the hell does he think he is?'

Natalya thrust the phone back into her bag and zipped the compartment.

He could wait.

She was hot, sweaty, in need of a shower and change of clothes following a vigorous hour of squash.

There was a sense of satisfaction in taking her time, and she emerged into the reception area to find Aaron waiting for her.

'Problem?'

'Is it that obvious?

'Uh-huh. You have *the look*.'

Natalya rolled her eyes.

'Alexei,' he concluded. 'What does he want?'

'I have no idea.'

'And you're not exactly in a hurry to find out.'

She sent him a faint smile. 'No.'

'Careful, sweetheart. Don't bite off more than you can chew.'

His concern was touching, and her expression softened. 'I'm no longer the vulnerable young girl of five years ago.'

'Nor is he the same man.'

Isn't that the truth.

A faint shiver slid down her spine, only to be instantly dispelled as they exited the building and crossed to the adjoining car park.

'Thanks for the game,' Natalya voiced as they reached her BMW.

'But not the advice.'

'That, too.'

Aaron placed a hand on her shoulder. 'Travel carefully.'

She deactivated the car's locking system, and sent him a sunny smile as she slid in behind the wheel. 'Always.'

Asap equated to urgency. Yet she waited an hour

before making the call. Justifying the delay as a need to stop by the food mart for grocery supplies, unpacking and depositing same into her fridge and pantry.

'Your smartphone was on charge; you failed to check for messages,' Alexei pre-empted with undisguised dryness as he picked up on the second buzz. 'Or was the delay merely sheer bloody-mindedness?'

'Good morning to you, too,' she offered with incredible politeness.

Strike one for Natalya.

'Afternoon.'

She made a play of checking her watch. 'By precisely three minutes,' she agreed. 'The nature of your call being?'

Was it possible for silence to be explosive? And why did the thought please her?

'A meeting set up in Melbourne late this afternoon. My car will collect you at three-thirty. You'll need an overnight bag.'

'Need I remind you it's the weekend? You expect me to drop everything at a moment's notice?'

'Yes.'

'And if I decline?'

'I suggest you reconsider.' His cool, slightly acerbic response hit a hot button, and she tamped down her temper.

Of course. He held all the cards in this diabolical game, with not one in her favour.

Once, just once she'd kill to be able to upset the balance of power between them.

Not going to happen anytime soon…

'Could we make it three forty-five?' Fifteen minutes was a small concession, albeit a deliberate one.

'No.'

Well, there you go. Nice try, even if it failed. With that, she slipped into smooth professional mode. 'Any specific instructions?'

Alexei outlined them with succinct brevity and ended the call.

Hotel. Restaurant. Six for seven. Suitable attire.

Natalya extended the tip of her tongue in an unladylike gesture, then she swept into her bedroom to pack.

CHAPTER EIGHT

HIGH-END MELBOURNE HOTEL, stunning river and inner-city views, *check*.

Top floor restaurant, good table, time and number of guests, *check*.

Luxury two-bedroom suite, each with en suite bathroom, and separated by lounge, *reluctant check*. A familiar business arrangement when travelling as Roman's PA.

However Alexei was not her father.

'I'd prefer a separate suite on the same floor.'

Alexei's eyebrow rose. 'On what grounds?'

She had a few, only one of which she was prepared to voice. 'Privacy.'

The faint lift at the edge of his mouth was so fleeting, she wondered if she'd merely imagined it.

'Afraid, Natalya?'

'Of you?' Her gaze met his with cool equanimity. 'Not in this lifetime.'

'In that case, I don't perceive there to be a problem.' He checked his watch. 'Order coffee in ten. Bring your iPad.' With that he collected his bag and disappeared into the bedroom on his right.

She ordered room service, took the second bedroom, freshened up, unpacked, and re-emerged into the lounge to find him seated at a desk checking data on his laptop.

He'd removed his suit jacket and tie, released the top few buttons of his shirt, and bore a raw masculinity that tugged at her nerve-ends, heated her blood and made her aware of every breath she took.

Not fair. Any of it.

Coffee arrived, and she filled both cups, placed one within Alexei's reach, opened her iPad and went to work keying in minor and a few major alterations to contractual clauses, highlighting the changes, then sent the amended contract to Alexei's laptop and checked the evening's schedule.

Four guests…three men well known in the electronics field and a PA.

There was time to shower, change into black silk evening trousers, attend to her make-up, style her hair, then slip on a stunning red jacket with matching silk lapels. A simple gold chain at her neck, small gold ear studs, a solid gold bracelet and her watch completed jewellery. Killer black Louboutins, and she was ready to go.

At six-fifty, evening purse tucked beneath her arm, satchel in hand, she emerged into the lounge to join Alexei.

Sensation arrowed deep within her as he turned to face her, and she had no control over the heat warming her body, or the way her pulse thudded to a quickened beat.

There was nothing classical about his features. Cheekbones a little too wide, the jawbone strong and emphasised by dark close-clipped designer stubble. Broad forehead, and eyes so dark they were almost black...equally expressive and warm, or cold as Russian ice. A generous beautifully moulded mouth, groomed hair a little longer than the current conventional style, a lithe toned body, an inherent air of power, success.

Unequivocally the *wow* factor.

So what?

She'd come into contact with equally attractive men. Yet none affected her the way Alexei had... *and still did.*

An admission she refused to give the slightest consideration.

Moving right along. They had a business dinner to attend, undoubtedly a late evening ahead, and any delays could lead to a further meeting the next day.

Superb food, splendid views of a stunning nightscape. Tall brightly lit city buildings, neon billboards...and skilled high-powered business as Alexei outlined his terms for a proposed deal involving one of ADE's subsidiary companies.

Interesting and slightly amusing to intercept the occasional glance aimed at Alexei by the super efficient blonde PA, a hint of sultry in her smile, the slow sweep of perfect mascara-enhanced lashes. Little doubt an attempt to signal discreet interest.

Like she *cared* if Alexei returned it? Natalya determined, and focussed on the job at hand.

The conglomerate represented by the three men

wanted concessions written into the existing contract, which Alexei refused to consider.

Negotiations moved up a notch, Natalya acknowledged as she declined a second glass of wine in favour of sparkling mineral water.

Power became an effective sword, one which Alexei chose to wield with ruthless purpose, resulting in the spokesman for the group making a calculated attempt over coffee to regain some balance in the power play.

Without success, as Alexei brought the evening to a close by rising to his feet, inclined his head in dismissal, and silently signalled Natalya.

'Gentlemen.'

Obsequiousness was out, but Natalya detected a hint of silent back-pedalling as the head partner attempted to counter. 'We'll confer and contact you tomorrow.'

Alexei didn't hesitate. 'I have another meeting in the morning at nine.'

The implication was clear. Play ball on Alexei's terms, or not at all, Natalya reflected as they rode the elevator in silence, exited at their designated floor, and headed towards their suite.

A faint element of tension curled around her nerve-ends as he used the entry card to disengage the door and indicate she precede him into the lounge.

Professional, remember?

'Goodnight.'

It was easy to turn towards her chosen bedroom, and she was almost there, her hand extended towards the door handle when the sound of his voice caused her to pause.

'I want the evening's report accessible on my laptop by seven in the morning.'

It was all she could do not to grit her teeth. Instead, she turned towards him, inclined her head and added with sweet emphasis, 'An indication of tomorrow's agenda would help facilitate a workable schedule.' A fractional pause accelerated by a steady unwavering look lent intended emphasis. 'Seven-thirty?'

She could have sworn she glimpsed a flicker of amusement in those dark eyes, then it was gone.

'We'll confer over breakfast. Order room service for two at seven-fifteen.'

A minor concession… Whether she compiled the report tonight, or rose early to complete it was neither here nor there.

Without a further word she turned and walked towards the adjoining bedroom.

'Sleep well.' His faint drawl held a tinge of amusement.

Natalya didn't miss a beat as she spared him a glance over one shoulder as she entered her room. 'I always do.'

With that, she closed the door behind her, turned the lock, and silently pumped a fist in the air.

There was something eminently satisfying in having the last word.

A victory short-lived, Natalya conceded as business ruled their early morning breakfast.

A relaxed CEO, she perceived, with the top two buttons of his shirt undone, sleeves turned back, suit jacket spread over the back of his chair.

A casual look she silently assured she was perfectly comfortable with…and knew she lied.

Five years had added a few slight changes if one looked closely enough. Fine lines fanned out from the far corners of his eyes. Close-clipped designer stubble added a ruthless quality to his facial features… and she squashed the stray thought whether it would feel soft or slightly bristly on a woman's soft skin.

Are you insane?

Just…curious, she hastened silently, and filled her cup with coffee. It said much for her level of control that her hand remained perfectly steady. So what if she took the coffee black, strong and unsweetened for the maximum caffeine hit?

Cool, professional, as they ran an updated check on the day's schedule. Tight, Natalya perceived, with little wiggle room for any unforeseen delay.

Vastly different from the leisurely meals she'd shared with her father during his regime when the first business meeting of the day began with an extensive lunch and rarely concluded until late afternoon. Dinner inevitably morphed into a social event with a well-imbibed Roman generously picking up the tab.

Chalk and cheese, she perceived as she drained the last of her coffee, slid the iPad into her satchel, and waited dutifully as Alexei buttoned his shirt, fixed his tie before shrugging into his jacket.

Attired in a black pencil-slim skirt and fitted jade-coloured jacket, killer heels, she felt ready to deal with whatever the day would bring as she preceded Alexei from their suite.

It didn't help that the elevator doors opened to reveal an almost full occupant capacity entailing up close and personal contact with her nemesis. Nor did it aid an increased pulse-beat as unwanted awareness unfurled deep within.

Natalya stood rigidly still, consciously ensuring her breathing remained even, measured, and didn't pound to a rapid beat as it threatened to do.

In a few short seconds the elevator would reach ground level, release its passengers…and she'd be able to breathe normally again.

Did he have any idea how his presence affected her?

Or how hard she fought against it?

There were many reasons to hate him, and she did…vehemently. So why did the light musky drift of Alexei's cologne tease and heighten her senses?

His height and muscled frame proved a powerful force impossible to ignore. So, too, the sexual chemistry he managed to exude with little or no effort at all.

Five years ago she'd relished every stolen moment with him, no matter how brief. His touch, warmth of his smile, the knowledge of more, much more, as soon as they were alone. Did he remember, as she did? Wake in the night wanting, needing what they'd once shared?

Obviously not.

So who's the fool haunted by images of a past best forgotten?

You have a life…or at least she did have until Alexei reappeared on the scene.

Her relief was palpable as the elevator slid to a smooth halt, and she accompanied Alexei across the marble-tiled lobby to the black limousine and driver parked adjacent the hotel entrance.

Any hope she had of occupying the rear seat alone was dashed when Alexei slid in beside her, and she silently cursed his close proximity as the limousine cruised through city streets towards their destination.

'No last-minute instructions?' Natalya managed quietly, and incurred his measured glance.

'None.'

Okay. Time out from idle conversation. Which suited her just fine.

Instead she reflected on the meeting's key points, and the background research she had managed to glean on the major player in opposition.

An open mind, adhere with polite formalities, record all details from both parties…and become the quintessential PA.

In other words, be prepared for anything.

The limousine pulled into a semi-circular driveway and drew to a halt adjacent an impressive entrance lobby.

Showtime, Natalya accorded as they were met and led towards a bank of elevators, one of which transported them to a high floor where they were escorted to a designated boardroom.

There was a brief moment when Alexei's hand inadvertently brushed her arm, and she hated the way her pulse immediately quickened to a crazy beat.

In the name of heaven...*focus*.

The fact she did owed more to the experience of long practice, and she took her seat at the conference table, extracted the necessary iPad, and minirecorder.

Playing tough in the business arena was an art form Alexei had mastered with unfailing ease as he calmly stripped negotiations to a base level of take it or leave it. Something which didn't augur well, and resulted in harsh criticism of ADE CEO's tactics.

Cut-throat didn't come close. Although Natalya had to concede the methodology worked. A break for lunch involved food eaten in one of the hotel's private rooms...and a review of key points from the morning's meeting.

High-powered, with Alexei's unyielding stance, and his superb negotiation skills.

Natalya could only quietly admire his ability to figuratively pin his business competitor to the wall... while her personal jury remained out regarding the inherent ruthlessness he managed to employ.

The pace increased during the afternoon, with Alexei adamant his terms were final, which led to a hastily arranged meeting the following morning.

'Reschedule our flight to mid-afternoon tomorrow,' Alexei instructed as their limousine took the route to their hotel.

Natalya sent him a killing look as they entered

their hotel suite. 'In this technological age legal documents can be digitally signed and emailed.'

'True.' He removed his suit jacket, loosened his
tie and tossed both onto a nearby chair as he sent her
a piercing look. 'You're questioning my decision?'

'Merely expressing an opinion.'

'Which you feel entitled to do?'

Why did she suddenly feel as if she'd ventured
onto shaky ground? 'It wasn't specifically mentioned
in my employment contract.'

Was that a faint gleam of humour in his dark gaze?

'Consult the menu and order a meal to be delivered
to our suite at seven.' Alexei waited a beat. 'I'll have
the seafood pilaf.' He reached forward and collected
his jacket and tie, then turned towards his room. 'I'll
change and go down to the gym for an hour.'

All this *togetherness* didn't augur well, especially
from her perspective. She could manage days, business lunches and dinners. It was the overnight thing
that bothered her. *Especially* the sharing of a suite,
despite it being a sensible business arrangement.

Hadn't she accompanied Roman to interstate meetings? Shared similar suites in several different hotels?

So why, now, did she feel wary? Defensive, on
edge?

Yet she did, and it angered her that she should.

Worse, a full-blown suspicion Alexei took pleasure in figuratively ruffling her feathers.

Civil during business discussions in the presence
of others, yet when alone with him she detected a

watchful element, almost as if he was deliberately intent on...*what*?

There had been a time when she could read him well. Yet the passing of time had wrought changes. Few of which she could condone. For even now, her heart ached for the loss of the love they'd once shared. The pain of him leaving her so suddenly without a word and no further contact, despite all her efforts, still existed...like a wound that had never completely healed.

So go do something constructive, an inner voice urged. *Check out the hotel boutiques. Or better yet, go swim laps in the hotel pool and work off some pent-up angst.*

The pool won out, and she quickly rang Room Service, placed an order, then retrieved a one-piece from her bag, changed, caught up a towelling robe, popped the suite swipe card into one of two capacious pockets, and took the elevator.

Most of the guests were readying themselves for drinks at the bar or in the lounge, and Natalya felt a sense of relief on discovering she had the pool to herself.

The water was enticing, crystal clear and sparkling. Without hesitation, she shrugged off the robe and dived in.

It felt so good as she rose to the water's surface and began stroking laps, one after the other, steady at first before picking up speed. After a while she lost count, content simply to power up and down the pool's length, varying strokes as the whim took her, until she simply rolled over and lazily backstroked to the pool's edge.

How long had she been in the water? Half an hour?

A quick glance at the wall clock revealed longer, and she hastily emerged, dried off, then pulled on the towelling robe. Ten minutes should be sufficient to return to the suite, shower and dress before room service delivered their evening meal.

Alexei was already seated in one of the lounge chairs as she entered the room, and she met his gaze, rolled her eyes, lifted a hand in a silent gesture and hurried towards her bedroom.

Oh, hell, emerged as a silent condemnation as she caught a glance at her mirrored reflection. Bright lights enhanced her damp hair...rats' tails was an apt description...bare face...great!

So what? He's seen you in less...a lot less. But that was years ago when things between them had been different.

Way different.

Suck it up, girl. Take the fastest shower ever, dress and wind wet hair into a knot on top of your head, add lip gloss and go.

Food, perhaps a shared wine, followed by coffee and a recap of the day's business at hand. An hour, maybe two. Then she could escape to her room, duty successfully executed for the evening.

Three hours, slightly more to be exact, Natalya perceived, as she checked her laptop, read and discussed pertinent points, gave her opinion when asked, and provided a requested overview from her perspective.

'Honesty? Or circumspection?'

Alexei leaned back in his chair. 'Both.'

'They want the deal on their terms.'

She was good, he conceded, aware just how well she'd covered for her father during the past few years. Without her, Roman's business would have crashed and burned way before it had become vulnerable to a takeover.

Family loyalty…or desperation? Maybe both.

'Not going to happen.' A statement, no wiggle room.

Of course not. Alexei held the power, and was unafraid to use it.

'You've decided on a predetermined figure,' Natalya ventured. 'I imagine they will offer ten percent lower, then prepare for you to negotiate.'

'Astute.'

She inclined her head. 'Thank you.'

'Did your father request your opinion on any of his business dealings?'

Now there was a question. 'Occasionally.' In a befuddled alcohol-infused state, only to resort to something totally different in the light of day.

'Yet he rarely implemented them.'

The truth hurt, in more ways than one. At peak, Montgomery Electronics could have sold at almost double what ADE had paid for it. 'No.'

'Did you resent that?'

This was becoming upfront and personal. She was a daughter, not the son Roman envisaged Ivana would dutifully bear him.

'Is there a point to this?'

His eyes took on a watchful quality. 'It fills in a few blanks.'

She drained the coffee in her cup, closed her iPad and stood to her feet. 'I think we're done for the evening.'

Alexei silently commended her efficiency, enjoyed the challenge she presented…and wondered what it would take to crack the shell she'd erected to protect herself.

From him? Or men in general?

It shouldn't bother him.

Yet it did.

She offered a polite goodnight and crossed the room to her bedroom suite.

'Sleep well.' His faintly mocking voice curled around her nerve-ends as she reached for the door handle.

What she wouldn't give to best him at something… anything, just for the satisfaction of doing so.

A feeling which continued as she undressed and made ready for bed, rearranged pillows and settled comfortably with a current paperback.

Two chapters, then she'd close the bed lamp and sleep.

Except an escape into blissful oblivion didn't appear to be happening anytime soon, as Alexei's compelling image filled her mind and refused to disappear, no matter how hard she fought to dispel it. Nor her ability to evade dreams of their shared past. The intimacies…erotic, all-encompassing, as she became alive beneath his touch in a mutual gift of passion in all its guises. Lost, so completely lost she had no recollection of anything other than Alexei.

Magical. Transcending to a place where heart, body and soul became one…until the dream began to fade into a reality where she slowly woke to discover her body damp with sensual heat. Bereft, wanting… with silent tears slowly drifting down her cheeks.

Her breath hitched for a second before she caught hold of the now, and the need to shower, dress and face the day ahead. As well as the man who managed to slip through her subconscious and invade her heart.

Their shared morning breakfast was interrupted by the ring tone of Alexei's smartphone, and Natalya lifted her head to witness his eyes darken.

Trouble?

Undoubtedly, as Alexei's voice hardened during a conversation with, she assumed, a spokesman representing the group with whom they'd shared dinner the previous evening.

It didn't sound promising, as Alexei firmly refused to consider any further negotiation.

He ended the call, calmly drained the rest of his coffee and refilled his cup. 'They've requested a two-hour extension. A delay with their bank.'

'In a bid to gain more time.' She made it a statement, not a question.

And you have no intention of playing into it, Natalya conceded. Nor would I, in your position. 'So we wait.'

We…a slip of the tongue, and a throwback to the days when she prompted her father, whenever he required it…more frequently than it should have been.

'They have my number, flight departure time,' Alexei stated. 'The ball is in their court.' He checked his watch. 'I'm catching up with a friend for an hour or two. During which time I need you to complete a few shopping items on my behalf.'

Natalya's eyes widened. 'Shopping?'

'Is that a problem?' There was a hint of wry amusement in his voice, and she met his gaze, held it.

'I gather you intend to supply a list?'

'Note it will be business combined with family while we're in New York,' he enlightened, as she retrieved her iPad.'

Natalya attempted to ignore the slight blip in her heartbeat, and stilled the temptation to tell him to choose his own gifts.

Yet if she displayed the slightest hesitation…

'I guess I can add it to my job description.' Just don't make a habit of it, she added silently. Helping the boss choose family gifts came under personal… and personal wasn't ever going to be in the picture.

'Your mother?'

'Books.'

'That's really not helpful,' Natalya offered. 'Fiction? Fact? Romance…modern, historical, suspense, crime? Shall I elaborate further?'

'Romantic suspense.'

This could go on for a while. 'Favourite authors?

Or don't you know?' She named a few, which presumably didn't strike a chord.

'Scarves,' he added. 'To add to my mother and sister-in-law's existing collection.'

'Any particular designer?'

He named a few, then handed over a credit card.

Safe choices, Natalya mused, and two hours later she had acquired numerous gifts beautifully wrapped and placed in a clutch of glossy carrier bags.

Ignoring the occasional brief...very brief moment, she recalled other occasions of shared shopping excursions. A time when Alexei would place an arm across her shoulders and catch her body close to his own. The dark emotion evident in his eyes, and the silent promise of how the day would end.

The memories shouldn't affect her...except they did, and she mentally struggled to put them back into a figurative box, and throw away the key.

She re-entered the hotel foyer to find Alexei standing to one side, newspaper in hand as he appeared seemingly engaged in reading an article.

Alexei's smartphone beeped as she drew close, and he moved aside to take the call, kept it brief while Natalya checked her watch, noted they had an hour and a half to pack, check out, and reach the airport to make their flight.

'The deal has been accepted,' Alexei relayed as he returned to her side.

Of course, she acknowledged silently. Had there been any doubt?

CHAPTER NINE

A FEW HOURS later they disembarked at Sydney's major airport, collected their bags, and were met by Paul in the passenger lounge.

'Welcome back,' Paul greeted with a smile. 'A successful trip?'

Natalya inclined her head as Alexei answered in the affirmative as Paul took hold of their bags, and began leading the way towards the exit.

Confirmation documents digitally signed in ADE Conglomerate's favour had been recorded. Another deal settled, Natalya acknowledged as Paul eased Alexei's limousine away from the terminal.

No matter how many domestic and international flights Natalya had made over the years, the return to Sydney inevitably invited the pleasure of familiarity, the buzz of city traffic, famous landmarks.

Mission accomplished, she acceded...admitting it was good to be back. Within half an hour of her own home, free of an insidious awareness pervading her senses with every passing day.

A temporary madness, she dismissed, due to being

in Alexei's presence a minimum of eight hours five days a week...more, if you counted business dinners, travel.

She didn't feel comfortable with it. Didn't condone he had managed to manoeuvre her between a rock and a hard place by robbing her of choice...aware there was only *one* choice she could make.

It made her want to rail her fists against him... except she didn't *do* tantrums. Couldn't remember throwing any, even as a child. Not that there had ever been a reason for her to do so.

A faint smile curved the edges of her lips. Except one incidence as a child in first grade when a boy... she couldn't even recall his name...grabbed hold of her single hair braid and pulled it so hard her eyes had watered. The taunt of 'cry-baby' had made her so mad she didn't hesitate to kick him...inadvertently where it hurt him most. An act which earned both children a demerit point, a lecture, and a phone call to each of their parents.

A forgotten incident...until now.

The limousine eased to a halt outside her home, and she emerged from the door Alexei held open while Paul removed her bag.

It was a simple expedient to offer Paul a polite word in thanks, reach for her bag, only to have Alexei collect it and accompany her to the front door, wait as she extracted her keys.

'I can take it from here.'

For a brief moment she imagined she glimpsed a tinge of amusement in his dark eyes. The temptation to execute an expressive eye-roll was uppermost. She selected the appropriate key, unlocked the front door, reached for her bag…missed by a mere second or two as Alexei placed it in the hallway before exiting without so much as a backwards glance.

An unladylike swear word slipped quietly from her lips, followed by another as she transferred her bag into her bedroom, tossed her satchel, then dug out her smartphone and rang Ben.

'Okay if I call over and collect Ollie?'

'Sure. He's antsy. I think he heard the car and your key in the door.'

'On my way.'

And there was Ben waiting for her with Ollie in his arms. 'Good trip?'

The fluffy cream seal-pointed cat squirmed with delight at the sight of his mistress, purred as Ben transferred him to Natalya, and she smiled as Ollie smooched his head into the curve of her neck, lightly nipped her earlobe in mild protest at her absence and followed it with another smooch.

'You missed me, huh?' Natalya acknowledged, and received a soft plaintive meow in return.

'Thanks, Ben. I appreciate you taking care of him.'

'No problem. Any time.'

He was a great neighbour, and looked out for her like the brother she didn't have. 'We'll catch up. Soon,' she added, meaning it.

'No rush. Whenever.'

She smiled, aware his life was even more hectic than her own. 'We're good.' And they were, for the pet

minding thing was reciprocal… Ben owned an ador-
able sad-faced pug named Alfie, whom she looked
after on occasion. 'Talk soon.'

'Look forward to it,' Ben bade as she crossed to
her adjoining apartment.

Time spent with Ollie, smooches, head-butts…
the feline equivalent of an adoring, *Welcome home.
I missed you*, and food…always a clincher.

After which she changed into comfortable sweats,
unpacked her bag, set up her laptop, checked the
agreement, itemised the salient points and sent
the data to Alexei. Resisting adding an expressive
emoji…only to send it separately minutes later.

Time for a light meal, shower, then hit the bed
with Ollie curled up beside her, maybe view a tele-
vision programme.

Surprisingly she slept well, woke early, checked
her email…no response from Alexei…then fed Ollie,
collected the morning newspaper, made breakfast,
then she poured a second cup of coffee and began
skimming the daily headlines.

Normally she might have missed the article, except
the bold print caught her eye. So, too, did the capi-
talised name—ADE CONGLOMERATE SCORES
MEGA DEAL—together with a photograph of ADE's
CEO, followed by brief details.

An approved press release from ADE? Doubtful,
given she would have known about it. Unauthorised,
damage control would ensue via a statement from
Alexei in the late afternoon news.

Exactly as Natalya predicted, followed by a phone

call from her father voicing a conspiracy rant, insisting she must have had advance knowledge the deal was about to go public. Concluding with a spiel alluding to the victory should have been his.

Any attempt to defuse the situation proved unsuccessful, and Natalya simply concluded the call, aware a reality check would prove a wasted effort.

Their return resulted in invitations to social events supporting various prominent charities arrived, requesting Alexei Delandros' presence and partner.

Back in the day of Roman's excesses and largess, almost all such invitations were accepted, including Natalya's attendance with her parents from the age of eighteen when she'd adapted to sharing the glitz and glamour as the social elite worked the ballroom.

Natalya checked each of the invitations, listed a few she warranted would benefit from Alexei's presence and probable donation, and placed them on his desk.

'I'll organise for an acceptance when you've made your choice.'

Would he decide to appear solo…and if not, whom would he choose as his partner?

Like she cared?

Yet deep down she did, and for a brief few seconds she considered attending with her parents…just *because*.

Only to have the decision taken out of her hands when Alexei summoned her into his office prior to an event.

Natalya took a seat, opened her iPad with her fingers poised to tap in an update, schedule or reschedule a meeting…and glanced up when he failed to begin.

It was the end of the day, and he'd removed his jacket, loosened his tie, aiding a casual look that succeeded in ruffling her composure.

'Ensure you're available for Thursday evening's charity event,' Alexei began.

She schooled her expression and met his steady gaze. 'I'm sure you have a few young women on speed dial who would jump at the chance of an invitation.'

'None of whom possess your observation skills and diplomacy.'

'Assuming their total focus would be on charming *you*?' Natalya queried sweetly, sure she caught a faint smile at the edge of his mouth.

'Consider your presence a necessity as my PA.'

Be seated at his side throughout a lengthy dinner? Play nice, when privately she wanted to hit him? An inconceivable action in public view. Something more subtle…an elbow in his ribs, perhaps? *Accidentally*, of course.

'Business-oriented,' she clarified in droll tones. 'I'll ensure the mini-recording device will fit in my evening purse.'

'You've attended several events in the past. I doubt tomorrow evening's event will be any different.'

A number of the people present were repeat guests at several of the city's charity events throughout each year. Wealthy, influential, dedicated in donating funds to worthy causes, active on the social scene…

and most familiar with Roman Montgomery's fall from grace in the finance sector.

The fact Roman's daughter would be seated next to, and to all intents and purposes partnered by, Alexei Delandros would be viewed with interest and a degree of speculation.

Poise and sophistication were an acquired façade, and qualities in which Natalya excelled...on the surface. Education in one of Sydney's highly respected private schools and world travel had ensured she could handle almost any situation without falling in a heap.

This evening's charity event would be no different. So why the edgy onset of nerves as she put the finishing touches to her make-up prior to Alexei's timed arrival at her home?

Her expressed insistence she meet him at the hotel venue had been dismissed out of hand, and for twenty-four hours she'd considered defying his edict with a last-minute text...only to abandon the tempting plan.

Instead she visited one of her favoured boutiques and purchased a new gown in champagne silk with an overlay of matching lace.

Dressed to kill, she observed as she added a diamond pendant on a slim gold chain, attached a single diamond tennis bracelet to her left wrist, adding discreet diamond ear studs...each of which had been gifts over time from her late grandmother.

Natalya ran her fingers over her hair, plumping the loose waved tendrils touching each collarbone, and reached for her evening purse.

Good to go, with a few minutes to spare.

Alexei's limousine slid to a halt at the prearranged time, and she drew in a deep breath as the doorbell rang.

Nervous tension, Natalya excused, and sought to steady the increased pulse-beat at the base of her throat as she opened the door.

He had presence, an elusive quality that set him apart from most other men. Difficult to define in mere words, but there nonetheless.

Dark eyes that could sear the soul; a mouth which held the promise of sensual sin…and delivered.

Stop, a silent voice echoed inside her brain. Remembering how it had been between them served no purpose.

As an escort he ticked all the boxes. Appearing even more devastating in impeccable evening wear, he could easily have passed as a male model in a photo shoot for Armani. The epitome of the man he'd become…assured, comfortable in his own skin. The acquisition of the fine things in life, its influence and power. An added quality he bore with ease.

The limousine purred silently through the city streets, entering the inner city perimeter until they reached the hotel where the evening's event was being held.

Assembled media, photographers were positioned ready to capture the arrival of well-known guests, and flashbulbs popped as the cream of Sydney's society descended from a moving procession of limousines… women offering practised smiles, should their photograph be one of a chosen few to make the following day's social pages.

Alexei's light touch at the back of Natalya's waist was a courtesy, although only she was aware of the flare of sensual electricity coursing through her body.

Her role was strictly business-oriented. Definitely not personal. She should have organised a pin discreetly emblazoned with PA to clarify her presence.

Natalya offered a slight smile as she accompanied Alexei into the large atrium where guests were gathering for pre-dinner drinks prior to a bank of doors being opened to allow access into the formal dining room.

Waiters circled the atrium offering flutes of champagne as guests mingled with fellow associates and friends, increasing the noise factor as the numbers swelled to capacity.

Natalya offered a smile in silent acknowledgment as she recognised friends among the crowd, aware they'd be able to connect throughout the evening, and when a few scions of industry approached Alexei she achieved each introduction with practised ease.

It became increasingly obvious Alexei garnered attention. His takeover of Roman Montgomery's firm had become a lingering buzz among those in the financial sector, fired by successful deals Alexei had achieved worldwide.

There was media interest in his background, together with any information investigative journalists could dig up about his personal life.

Until now Alexei had declined to give interviews, sanctioning only information his media personnel were instructed to release. Fine in theory, but the gutter press possessed few scruples, and a grain of truth embellished with innuendo could increase sales of varying tabloids tenfold.

'Natalya.' The sound of Ivana's voice captured her attention, and she greeted her parents with affection, formally introduced Alexei to her mother, who offered him a gracious smile and shook his hand.

'You've already met my father,' Natalya indicated, sensing the tension beneath the obsequious smile as Roman extended his hand.

'Indeed,' Roman expressed. 'So pleased you've taken Natalya on board. She's an excellent PA.'

Proficient at covering your back...words which remained silent.

'Ivana, darling. We're seated together.' Aaron's mother, Elvira, Natalya perceived, aware both women were long time friends. 'Roman. Natalya.' Her gaze shifted towards Alexei. 'Alexei Delandros, of course. You photograph well. I'm delighted to meet you.' She turned towards Natalya. 'Aaron is parking the car. Al has been shanghaied by a client. I'm sure he'll manage to escape soon.'

Interesting didn't begin to describe the seating arrangement. Aaron, the gay son whose parents were in ignorance of their son's sexual proclivities; Alexei and Roman...which member of the committee thought to put the fox and the rabbit together? Each table seated twelve. Who were the remaining five?

'Ah, they're opening the doors,' Elvira declared. 'Shall we go in?'

Moving within a crowd involved some inadvertent contact with other patrons, and she stiffened as Alexei placed an arm along the back of her waist... and kept it there until they reached their table, choosing to position her chair as she graciously took a seat. The gesture polite, impersonal...so why did his touch affect her body as much as it did?

A temporary madness, and one which she'd avoid by maintaining a reasonable distance between them. Which worked until a complement of five guests soon joined them. None other than Lara and Richard Tremayne, their two daughters Abby and Olivia, with son Jason bringing up the rear.

Like she needed *awkward*?

Nothing she couldn't handle...and she did, with grace and politeness, expressing amusement at the right intervals, while easing her way through three courses of beautifully presented delectable food.

'Champagne, Natalya?' Alexei queried, and she spared him a polite smile.

'Thank you.'

Definitely a departure from her usual preference of sparkling mineral water, and she caught Aaron's faintly raised eyebrow in silent askance.

On the surface all twelve patrons at their table appeared to be sharing a pleasant evening. Perhaps they were, and she was the only one present who sensed an edge of tension.

It was a relief when the wait-staff began clearing

tables in preparation for serving coffee. An action which usually pre-empted a series of announce-ments, speeches offering thanks for generous do-nations, the evening's success, followed by music and the voiced encouragement for guests to enjoy the dance floor.

Roman stood to his feet and crossed to Natalya's side and extended his hand. 'Shall we?'

At least her father employed a little circumspec-tion in leading her part-way through the waltz before he lowered his head a little and quietly demanded,

'What in hell are you thinking?'

She didn't pretend to misunderstand. 'I'm Alexei's PA, and seated with him in a professional capacity.'

'Darling girl, he's merely using you to highlight his success over my business failure.'

Natalya looked at him, glimpsed the anger, the frustration evident, and sought to alleviate it. 'Why would he do that, when the media have already printed the coup in various newspapers?'

Roman snorted in derision. 'Didn't you learn any-thing five years ago? The man upped and left you without a word.'

'That's not relevant to the current discussion.' Her voice was firm as she refused to placate him. 'Shall we rejoin the others?'

Coffee, hot, black, with no sugar helped, Natalya admitted, and she offered a smile as Roman swept her mother onto the dance floor, which left Natalya, Alexei and Jason Tremayne the only occupants at the table.

Not the best scenario, she perceived, wondering if she could escape to the powder room. However luck wasn't on her side as Jason rose to his feet and approached her.

'Our turn, I think.'

'Mine actually,' Alexei intervened smoothly as he rose to his feet and placed a hand on her shoulder. 'If you'll excuse us?'

She could refuse him, plead the need for a coffee refill, and attempt to relax. Instead she inclined her head towards Jason, offered a faint smile, and accompanied Alexei onto the dance floor.

'That wasn't necessary,' Natalya said quietly as she matched his steps with familiar ease.

'No?'

What could she say? If in doubt, don't, and in this instance silence was the better option.

The music slowed, and Alexei pulled her in as they adjusted their steps to a softer beat. The top of her head barely reached his shoulder, and he fought the urge to wrap an arm around her slender body, brush his lips to her temple…as he had done in the past. Enjoy the light floral perfume she wore, aware of his body pulsing with need, and the promise of how the night would end.

He'd been so sure of their relationship, of *her*, envisaging they'd grow old together, having raised a family, and enjoy grandchildren. Until Roman Montgomery had employed strong-arm tactics to ensure Alexei's swift departure from Sydney *and* the country.

Five years on, Alexei had changed, so too had his life.

The human psyche had intrigued him to such a point whereby he'd studied psychological behavioural patterns, mannerisms, characteristics that would provide insight to figurative red flags during his business dealings.

Qualities that had led to his success.

Had it hardened him? Undoubtedly.

His late father would have been proud.

'We should return to the table,' Natalya indicated as the music sped up to a modern beat. 'Considering the duty dance is done.'

'Duty?' Alexei queried as he released her. 'Is that what it was?'

'Of course,' she dismissed. 'What else would it have been?'

Indeed. If he hadn't noted the fast-beating pulse at the base of her throat, felt the throb of it beneath the palm of her wrist, he might have believed her.

The evening eventually drew to a close, with the final speech, the lucky door ticket prize, with guests lingering in the adjoining atrium as they waited for taxis, private limousines, while others continued on to a nightclub.

There were hugs, air kisses, voiced promises to do lunch or coffee…the usual pattern following the end of an evening's social event.

'The limousine will be here within a few minutes,' Alexei indicated.

'I can easily take a cab.'

'But you won't.'

Her lips parted with the intention of arguing with him, only for her to decide against it. Besides, taxis at this time of night were in short supply.

'Compliance, Natalya?'

She spared him a glance. 'Only because it makes sense.'

And if you *dare* smile…

He didn't, or else she missed it as Paul eased the limousine to a halt at the kerb. The late evening flow of traffic was intense as patrons vacated cinemas, cafés and restaurants until they cleared the inner city and crossed the harbour bridge.

'I trust you both enjoyed a pleasant evening?' Paul queried, and it was Alexei who responded,

'Successful.'

The context had to relate to the capacity crowd, donations raised, and Natalya added, 'Very much so.'

There was a sense of relief when the limousine drew to a halt in her driveway, her set of keys in hand as she released the door clasp and stepped out in one fluid movement, pausing to offer, 'Thanks for the ride, the evening.' She held up her set of keys. 'I'm fine. My porch light is on a timer.' She closed the rear door, then turned towards the gated path, unaware Alexei had joined her.

'I'm quite capable of walking unaccompanied to my front door.'

'I was unaware I implied otherwise.' His voice was a musing drawl, and she was conscious of the sharp tug of awareness, the unbidden heat flooding her body…and silently damned her own vulnerability, choosing to glance at the lit window on the far left of the house.

'You share the house with someone?'

Not an unusual question, given its spacious size.

'It's a large family home divided in half to incorporate two separate units. I occupy one. Ben leases the other.'

Alexei's eyes narrowed. He had no recollection of her mentioning anyone by that name. And he would have. A sharp memory was one of his talents. 'Since when?'

'Two and a half years ago.' She deactivated security, then inserted her key into the lock and heard Ollie's pathetic wail. 'My cat,' she enlightened as she opened the door, whereupon Ollie leapt into her arms and began purring as he affectionately butted his head against her chin.

Feline love, gifted unconditionally. If only human emotions were as uncomplicated…

Except they weren't, and Natalya offered Alexei a polite goodnight, entered the spacious hallway, then with a brief smile she closed and locked the door. Less than a minute later the veranda light faded, and she released her breath.

'Bed, hmm,' she murmured against Ollie's furry head. But sleep came without success, as she tossed and turned for what seemed an hour or more, only to check the illuminated hands on her watch to witness only thirty minutes had gone by.

Ollie protested and resettled his furry self at the base of the bed as Natalya punched her pillow, counted to ten, and sought a more comfortable position.

But there were too many images filling her mind of the times when she and Alexei were so attuned to each other there had been no need for words. Magical, engaging, special…so much so, she would have wagered her life nothing, no one, could tear them apart.

Yet someone or something had.

CHAPTER TEN

NATALYA MUST HAVE SLEPT, for when she woke Friday morning the sun was filtering through the bedroom shutters, and a quick glance at the bedside clock revealed she had plenty of time to shower, dress, linger over breakfast, flip pages through the daily newspaper and feed the cat, ready to face whatever the day might bring.

But something in the press changed her light mood to one of outrage as she caught a newsprint photo on the social page featuring Alexei handing her into his limousine. Taken on angle the photographer had managed to imply an intimacy that didn't exist.

Worse, the caption—MOGUL AND FORMER LOVER TOGETHER AGAIN?—was endorsed by a brief paragraph beneath the photo.

Without hesitation she tore out the page, folded it and thrust it into her satchel.

Seconds later the phone rang, and she bit back an unladylike curse as she saw the ID.

'Hi, Dad.'

That was as far as she got, before her father launched

into a diatribe, which in essence demanded to know what was going on between her and Alexei.

Soothing him down took several minutes, until she cut his words short with the excuse she had to leave for work.

She was barely a kilometre from her apartment in heavy morning traffic when her cell phone beeped with an incoming text.

WTH? Aaron.

Her staunch and loyal friend who'd supported her through the worst of times had clearly seen the same photograph too.

Worse, she garnered a few speculative glances as she rode an elevator to the high floor occupied by ADE Electronics.

All it took was one vigilant employee to start the gossip mill…and who better the focus than Natalya Montgomery, daughter of the fallen Roman Montgomery *and* former lover of the new head honcho, Alexei Delandros?

Dammit. This had to be stopped *now.*

She ignored her own office and in one swift action she retrieved the newsprint page and marched directly into Alexei's office…which probably wasn't the best idea, but she was so angry she didn't care.

If he was surprised, he failed to show it, and she hated that he'd leaned back in his chair seemingly intent on regarding her with detached interest as she crossed to his desk.

Natalya drew in a deep breath, then released it slowly. 'Let's get one thing straight,' she stated firmly. 'I'll act the polite efficient PA in all matters business. Anything alluding to *personal* is off the table.'

He waited a beat. 'Clarify *personal*?'

'Placing me in an invidious position.'

'Apropos of?'

Natalya extracted the page she'd torn from the daily newspaper and placed it on his desk. *'This.'*

She watched as he skimmed the offending caption…and waited for his reaction. Except there was none.

'I have no control over the media's agenda.'

Had the light touch of his hand at her waist been deliberate? Or was she simply being super-sensitive?

It irked he had the power to tie her emotions in knots… She hated that she actively looked for and subsequently judged his every word and action, silently seething if she imagined they crossed the line… *her* self-imposed line.

Her eyes darkened measurably. 'I want a retraction printed in tomorrow's edition.'

Alexei leant further back in his chair and regarded her thoughtfully. 'Don't you think that will only exacerbate the situation?'

Natalya drew a deep breath, then released it as her eyes darkened with anger. 'There is no *situation*.'

He lifted one eyebrow. 'Perhaps you'd care to inform the media of that?'

She pursed her lips, then opened her mouth to deliver a volley of words best left unsaid. Instead she

directed him a glare which had no visible effect whatsoever, much to her annoyance, leaving her little option except to turn on her heel and sweep out from
his office.

Her silent frustration with the media's intrusion
continued throughout the morning, while she fought
to qualify they were only doing their job. Not that
it helped much. Nor did she feel comfortable with a
part of her private life being played out in the public domain.

Natalya ordered lunch in, despatched a text to
Ivana, and cursed beneath her breath when Reception notified several calls representing the media had
not been redirected to Alexei Delandros' PA.

Like she *needed* this?

Late afternoon a text arrived on her smartphone.

Flight Monday a.m. Sydney/NY. Details laptop. Confirm. Alexei.

Two weeks? Natalya silently queried when she
checked her laptop and read Alexei's schedule.

The expected meetings, a few business lunches,
three business dinners. Family.

Alexei's family. So, not all business.

Which meant she'd have free time to check out a
few upmarket boutiques, enjoy a leisurely coffee in
any one of numerous cafés. Me time.

She sent off a text in confirmation, then she turned
her chair towards the plate-glass window, momentarily took in the harbour view, and smiled.

Suddenly the day appeared a little brighter.

The weekend involved a close inspection of her wardrobe, a list of items to pack, the need to check with Ben if he could look after Ollie, a phone call to Ivana, who listened, wisely chose to relay a simple, 'Take care, darling,' instead of a litany of words attributed to caution of the personal kind. So not Ivana's style.

When the persistent beep of the alarm woke her the next morning, Natalya had an urge to push the off button, roll over and grab another hour's sleep, only to groan…*not going to happen.*

There was a need to be ready on time. Alexei's text stating she be ready for pick-up at seven-thirty a.m. ensured she was waiting on the front veranda with her luggage, overnight bag and satchel.

Sure enough the limousine slid to the kerb with Paul at the wheel. Within minutes the driver transferred her luggage while she joined Alexei in the rear passenger seat.

'Good morning.' Pleasant, she could do pleasant… which he responded to in like manner.

There was no need to run through their immediate agenda. They could do that once they were in the air.

Not a passenger jet, Natalya discovered, but a private one. Expensive, luxurious and essentially an office in the air with cabin staff who provided coffee, offered a light meal be served once they reached cruising speed.

A review of their agenda required a few adjustments, and their first appointment in New York required only a minor amendment.

'There's a sleeping compartment with a comfortable bed adjoining the en suite bathroom,' Alexei relayed as he retrieved a set of earphones. 'I suggest you get a few hours' rest.'

'What about you?' The query was out before she'd given it any thought.

'I'll take the second shift.' He paused, and his eyes met her own. 'Unless you suggest we share?'

'Not going to happen.' Her response was instant, and his mouth curved a little.

'Relax, Natalya.'

She hadn't been able to completely relax since the first day he'd reappeared in her life.

The bedroom compartment was more spacious than she expected, containing a bed with fresh linens, a small wardrobe, appointed mod-cons, and a comfortable chair.

It took a few minutes to discard her outer clothes, remove make-up and don a wrap, then she turned back the bedcovers, settled comfortably, and much to her surprise she slept for more than four hours and woke feeling refreshed. Suitably clothed, she applied moisturiser, added a touch of colour to her lips, then she returned to the cabin, accepted fruit and coffee while Alexei sought the sleeping compartment.

Which became more restless than restful as the light floral perfume Natalya used lingered to taunt him with memories of shared passion, and what he'd believed to be unconditional love.

Elicited fact appeared to prove him wrong.

Yet deep in his gut there was a kernel of doubt based on the occasional unguarded moment during the past few weeks…when he was able to catch a glimpse of the young woman he'd known so well. A momentary warmth in her smile. A faint wistfulness, only for it to quickly disappear.

The slight change in her breathing when he'd held her in his arms on the dance floor. The tension evident in her stance when he escorted her to the front door of her home. There was a degree of vulnerability evident he found intriguing…a quality she endeavoured to disguise. And almost succeeded.

A stopover in Los Angeles for the jet to refuel, Customs, before boarding for the final leg of their flight to New York…where a uniformed chauffeur was waiting for them in the Arrivals lounge.

A service Alexei had obviously used on prior occasions, Natalya observed, given the ease of friendship between both men, and with smooth economy of movement their luggage was cleared from the carousel, carried through the terminal and deposited in the boot of a sleek black limousine which had slid smoothly to the kerb.

A driver *and* a bodyguard?

Elevated status…or a necessity?

New York contained a variety of differing vibes… from extreme wealth and luxury to the opposite end of the spectrum. Alive with a mix of cultures, from traditional to the exotic. A city which moved to a certain beat, glamour, pizzazz, to the bleakness of the Projects. A familiar vibe she recalled from previous business trips she had shared as her father's PA.

Music was key to the difference in attire and speech, and Natalya breathed it in as the limousine traversed the distance between airport to the high-end hotel in the vicinity of Central Park.

Classy, Natalya determined as they rode the elevator to a high floor, with stunning views over the city that never slept.

For the following few days they attended meetings, while maintaining a painstakingly professional façade.

Each day became mission accomplished. The nights, not so much.

Arranging business dinners didn't faze her, nor had attending them when the CEO had been her father. Alexei was someone else entirely.

Five years had wrought changes in Alexei she'd thought she'd known so well. Eyes dark, gleaming, sensual, conveying with just a look how the night would end.

The antithesis of the man he'd become…hardwired, ruthless—*driven*.

Except she was no longer the biddable young girl with stars in her eyes, imagining love would overcome everything.

How wrong had she been? she reflected as she dressed for the evening ahead. Formal, Alexei had forewarned, and she selected a red gown with a high neck artfully draped to cover each breast, leaving her shoulders and arms bare, nipped in at the waist to fall in a swirl of soft material at her feet. Subtle make-up, emphasis on the eyes, bold red lip gloss, her hair styled in large soft waves which fell past her shoulders and curved forward to partly frame her face, a touch of jewellery, she gathered up a wrap in matching red, slid her feet into red stilettos, took a deep breath, and emerged into the adjoining lounge to find Alexei conducting a conversation on his smartphone in a language she failed to comprehend.

Black evening suit, white shirt and black bow tie did much to emphasise his European features, impossibly dark eyes and wide mobile mouth. A mouth that could wreak mindless havoc...as she knew too well.

His cologne held a subtle blend of musk and something she failed to define...a soft sensual whisper that teased, taunted and made her think of the forbidden.

Each breath she took in his presence became measured, *controlled*, as every muscle in her body slowly tightened. In the close confines of the limousine she felt as brittle as the most delicate piece of Venetian glass.

One touch, and she'd shatter.

CHAPTER ELEVEN

THE EVENING AHEAD was a formal occasion. *Very* formal, Natalya noted, given the venue, the sumptuous grand dining room, the quality linen covering the many tables, exquisite crystal, cutlery and tableware.

Security was evident, invitations carefully checked, and guests personally escorted to their tables.

A gala event of note.

'Why me?' she had queried quietly, and incurred his studied look.

'Why not you?'

'This is social, not business.'

'The lines between the two are blurred, are they not?'

Anything else she might have added remained unsaid as a stunning blonde, who appeared out of nowhere behind him, snuggled close against his back, wound her arms around his neck.

'Guess who?'

Natalya caught a glimpse of diamond rings, a diamond necklace, sensed a drift of exotic perfume, heard the sultry in the young woman's voice, and felt her stomach plummet.

A friend? Lover? Mistress?

'Stassi,' Alexei acknowledged with a tinge of amusement as she released her hands and stepped to face him. 'Your signature perfume is unmistakable.'

There was a light tinkle of laughter followed by a staged *moue*…belied by the sparkle in Stassi's eyes as she stood on tiptoe to brush a light kiss to his cheek before turning towards Natalya. 'And you are?'

'Natalya,' Alexei drawled. 'Let me introduce you to my irrepressible cousin, Stassi.'

'Family,' Stassi declared. 'So Alexei is off limits, unfortunately. Although he does duty as a partner on occasion.' She glanced from Natalya to Alexei. 'And you are Alexei's…?'

'Friend,' Alexei declared.

'Uh-huh. Euphemism for…?'

'Friend,' he drawled, undeterred by his cousin's inquisitiveness.

'PA,' Natalya corrected.

Stassi smiled. 'Business *and* pleasure. Interesting combination.' She offered Alexei a teasing grin. 'You do realise your mother is planning a family dinner in your honour? She'll be delighted to welcome Natalya.'

Family? No, not happening. 'I don't think my presence would be appropriate.'

'Alexei will do his persuasive best,' Stassi stated with a light laugh. 'He's very good at it.' A slow smile curved her lips. 'I really must return to the parents. They have plotted to introduce me to a gorgeous man who, according to my darling mama, displays excellent potential as future husband material. Should be a fun evening.' She kissed her fingers and playfully touched them to Alexei's cheek. 'Take care.'

She turned towards Natalya. 'I'll look forward to catching up with you again.' With a mischievous smile she began threading her way through the numerous guests.

'Your cousin is delightful,' Natalya ventured politely, and caught his musing expression.

'Yes, she is. She's also intelligent, with a degree in criminal law. Loves life, has no intention of marrying, now or in the near future. Much to her mother's despair.'

'She obviously hasn't met the right man.'

'Is marriage so important?'

Sticky question, and not one Natalya was prepared to answer. Five years ago she would have said marriage represented a lifetime commitment, enduring love, growing a family…including qualities such as trust, faith and respect. Sharing the good and the not-so-good times together, without blame or regret.

'No comment, Natalya?'

She managed a credible smile. 'Much depends on one's life plan, don't you think?'

'And yours is?'

'Personal.'

For a moment she glimpsed a slight change in his expression, then it was gone, and she was left to ponder if her imagination was playing tricks.

'Perhaps we should take our seats,' Alexei indicated smoothly, inclining his head to a staff member waiting to escort them to their reserved table.

Society's glitterati at its finest, Natalya noted, as she sipped an excellent French wine. Similar to, but different from, she perceived, other charity functions she'd attended in the past. For there was ample evidence of extreme wealth apparent in the women's designer gowns, and their jewellery alone could have funded housing and food for a poor nation.

Cosmetic enhancement appeared to be *de rigueur* for the mature women, varying hairstyles combed and teased to within a whisper of perfection.

Nor, she suspected, was it confined to the women.

It was akin to viewing a movie on screen, where the majority of guests were actors playing a part, prepared by stylists, make-up artists, such was the achieved element of perfection.

The ballroom was enormous, and soon seated to capacity. Soft background music became almost lost to the chatter of voices as stylishly clothed wait staff ensured champagne and fine wines were replenished with reputed flair.

'Darling Alexei,' a female guest seated opposite at their table inclined with exquisite poise. 'I heard you'd touched down in this part of town.' All that was required to complete the woman's image was a long cigarette holder, for she had the pose down pat of the lead actress who played the original role of Auntie Mame in an old movie. 'So delighted you could grace us with your presence. But then, you have a vested interest in the nominated charity.' Her smile held graceful interest as it settled on Natalya.

'You've brought along an interesting new friend. Natalie, I believe?'

'Natalya.' It was easy to smile as she offered the correction.

'Of Russian origin?'

'It was my great-grandmother's name.'

'How interesting.'

Her great-grandmother's history *was* interesting... the story of a family who escaped a life of poverty to settle on a distant relative's farm in northern Europe. As a young girl of eighteen, she'd entered into an arranged marriage and bore four children...the youngest of which being Natalya's grandmother, who'd fled to America as a teenager, found work and lodging in a Californian vineyard, borrowed a sewing machine and made children's clothes long hours into the night. Embroidery was her specialty, and at first her exquisitely embroidered gowns sold by word of mouth, until she was encouraged to sell direct to a childrenswear shop in a nearby town. In storybook style, her grandmother had married the vintner's son, bore two children, a girl and a boy. Sadly her husband and young son were killed in an accident together with her husband's parents. Stricken with grief, Natalya's grandmother attempted to run the vineyard, only to sell it within two years, and start a new life with her daughter Ivana in Australia, settling in Sydney, where she set up shop, employed minimum staff, and gradually expanded over time to export her childrenswear overseas.

Natalya's cherished Babushka...so morally and

emotionally strong. A woman who had worked every day of her life and for whom family was everything, and who left behind so many memories of love, wisdom and laughter.

'More champagne?'

The sound of Alexei's voice intruded, and the ballroom with its numerous guests returned in sharp focus as Natalya offered a polite smile together with a quietly voiced refusal.

Background music faded, and there was the introductory speech of welcome, followed by the purpose of the charity in question, funds raised, together with a plea for guests to be generous with their donations.

In terms of success, the event topped the scale, given the plaudits offered throughout the evening. Guests appeared at their sparkling best, the food superb and the champagne flowed.

Polite small-talk appeared to be the order of the evening…the best party a few of the society doyennes had attended, who were present, snippets of gossip, and descriptions of apparel…designer of course, and who wore it best.

Different country, another major city…familiar scenario, merely on a larger scale.

Natalya briefly compared the evening with some she had attended with her father; the increasing tension as his alcohol intake rose, and her attempt to minimise the fallout. The relief when the evening came to a close and they could leave.

Now there was tension of a different kind, arising from her emotional reaction to Alexei's presence. Sexual sensuality…a heightened awareness that threatened her sanity. The question being…what was she going to do about it?

'We'll be dining at my mother's home this evening.' Alexei's seemingly normal statement following breakfast the next morning caused Natalya's breath to momentarily catch in her throat.

We?

Her fingers momentarily paused from keying words into her laptop.

Surely she'd misheard?

'I'm sure you'll enjoy spending time with her,' she offered with genuine sincerity as she set her fingers tapping on the keys.

There was a need to transcribe recorded notes from the previous day's meeting, prior to lunch and a mid-afternoon consult…when casual attire would be exchanged for suit, heels to present a more professional image.

Vastly different from his current casual attire of black fitted jeans and black tee shirt which emphasised the breadth of his shoulders, powerful flex of toned forearm musculature…the taut stomach, narrow waist and six-pack abs. The fact he worked out was evident in every move he made.

It made her want to explore. To track every muscle, the hard flex and tone with her hands. Purr with pleasure at the thought of dragging the tee shirt from his body, to tease and caress his bare skin…with the familiar touch of a lover.

Exult in his response, the faint catch in his breath when she unbuckled the belt at his waist, slid the studded button free, then slowly freed the zip of his jeans in a slow sensuous play that could only have one end…almost crying out as he mimicked each movement she made, slowly, with exquisite care. The almost reverent touch as he cupped each breast, lowered his head to taste one nipple, and drove her wild as he used his mouth to draw it deep and suckle, before slowly withdrawing to shift focus to its twin.

The way she trailed a hand over his stomach to trace the extended length of him, feel, rather than sense his indrawn breath, the shift in his body as he lifted his head and claimed her mouth in erotic possession…until extended foreplay wasn't enough. Nor the whispered words inciting the sensual promise of sexual pleasure.

Stop right there, a silent voice echoed in Natalya's mind. Mentally reliving an erotic memory of what they'd once shared served no purpose.

Almost as if Alexei knew, his dark eyes lifted and held her own for what seemed to be a long minute, when it could only have been a few seconds.

She couldn't move, nor did she have the power to utter a word.

A lost moment in time, brief…but it took an age before she managed to gather herself together and gain a sense of focus on the prosaic…laptop, transcribing notes.

Yet her mind lingered… Five years on there was a maturity evident, an innate knowledge of the man he had become. A certain ruthlessness apparent that almost alluded to an element of danger should anyone be sufficiently foolish to attempt to thwart him... on any level.

He possessed charm, respect, loyalty, and employed each characteristic facet with ease. Yet he possessed the ability to freeze an opponent with a mere glance; the power to walk away from a prospective deal without so much as a second's hesitation.

Was that how he treated his women?

Don't go there.

'The invitation includes you.'

Natalya's fingers inadvertently touched a wrong key, and a silent epithet echoed inside her head as she turned towards him.

Professional, she could manage. Sharing dinner with Alexei's mother was in a different category entirely.

'Will I be required to take notes this evening?' The query held polite civility, and one as his PA she was entitled to ask.

Alexei's expression remained unchanged. 'Possibly, given my two brothers and I form part of a European-based business partnership. Although primarily the evening will be a family gathering.'

Her stomach executed a slow roll of discomfort. She didn't do family...specifically not an ex-lover's family.

A slightly hysterical laugh rose and died in her throat. Like she'd had more than one lover?

A couple of close encounters that hadn't ended

well, when there had been the expectation of more than she was prepared to indulge.

'Given the evening is family-oriented, and any business matters are unlikely to be discussed on a level requiring my presence,' she inclined, 'I'll—'

'Pass?' Alexei lifted one eyebrow. 'My mother is expecting you. My sister-in-law will be delighted to have you there to tone down what she refers to as excessive male testosterone.' A faint smile curved the edges of his mouth. 'Despite qualifying affection for her two brothers-in-law.'

'I don't think it's appropriate.'

'What are you afraid of, Natalya?' His eyes held a glimmer of dark humour. 'We might be issued an invitation to stay overnight?'

In the same bedroom? How much of her former relationship with Alexei was his family aware of?

Almost as if he knew the passage of her thoughts, he offered quietly, 'Any fears you might have are completely groundless.'

Were they? So why this feeling of heightened awareness? She didn't want or need a reminder of what they'd once shared. She'd dealt with the past, moved on, created a pleasant life for herself.

Who do you think you're fooling?

'I agree,' she managed firmly. 'For each of us.'

Alexei moved in close before she had time to draw breath and laid his mouth over her own in what began as an explorative kiss that soon changed and became something else.

She wanted to protest, and lifted both hands to create a distance between them, only to have them falter as the years melted away as she was transported back to a place and time where everything was right between them.

She had no recollection of the passage of time... only the assault on her senses as he brought her emotions alive in a manner that tripped her heart into rapid beat.

Heaven, and then some, as she began to respond, uncaring at that moment where it might lead...and if it did, would she gain the emotional strength to step away?

Then he released her, and the room came into focus...together with reality.

There was a need to breathe in a conscious effort to still each throbbing pulse in her body...acutely sensitive to the once familiar touch personally geared to send her totally undone. As it had in the past.

'An experiment, Alexei?' She even managed to inject a shred of disdain into her voice, caught the dark glitter in his gaze before it was masked, and she valiantly ignored the sudden lump that rose in her throat.

There was only the heavy thud of her heartbeat as she sought to bring wildly swirling emotions under control. The words I hate you remained unsaid...*just*.

Or was it herself she hated? For momentarily succumbing to the special magic they'd once shared. And its vivid reminder.

'An answer.'

Which didn't sit well with her at all. 'You think?'

With forced calm she crossed to the mirror, extracted

her lipstick, repaired the damage, then she caught up her satchel, included her laptop, recording device, added sundry necessities…and moved towards the front door of their hotel apartment, all too aware of his close proximity as they rode the elevator down to lobby level. Prepared, in essence, to become the quintessential PA as business meetings were due to unfold for the day ahead.

CHAPTER TWELVE

Calista Delandros resided in an elite part of George-
town.

A slender elegantly attired woman who welcomed
her son with a warm hug, before extending a hand in
greeting to the young woman who stood at his side.

'Natalya. Welcome to my home.' Her smile was
genuine. 'The family are waiting in the lounge. Let's
join them, shall we?'

Beautifully appointed, fine handcrafted furniture, framed family pictures on the walls. Warm,
welcoming, Natalya perceived as Calista indicated a
large comfortably furnished lounge where two men
stood… Alexei's brothers, without doubt, given the
likeness in height, stature, and facial features. A
young woman displaying the slight emerging bump
of early pregnancy held the small hand of a young
girl.

'Cristos,' Alexei greeted and clasped his brother in
a brief hug before indicating, 'Cristos's wife, Xena,
and their daughter, Gigi. My younger brother, Dimitri.' He turned to include Natalya. 'Natalya. My PA.'

Natalya smiled…a smile was good. Polite, professional.

It was Xena's daughter who captured Natalya's attention. Petite, dark curls framing beautiful features, offering a smile to melt hearts.

'Gigi is a lovely name,' Natalya said gently.

She was rewarded with a polite, 'Thank you.'

For a few fleeting seconds it proved difficult to ignore the faint wistful ache in the region of her heart.

It was relatively easy to converse, to fit in, as the evening progressed. A skill she'd mastered since midteen years, together with an interest in current world affairs and a degree of genuine charm.

She accepted a small measure of wine, which she sipped as she observed family dynamics, their affection, and genuine interest in the current play in each of their lives.

Cristos headed the New York arm of the family business, while Dimitri travelled to interstate branches, and maintained an active social life…very social, Natalya surmised from the slightly wicked gleam in his eyes.

A family originating in Greece, as had Calista's late husband. Evident in some of the classical pottery on display in a few of the glass cabinets.

A faint lilt, not exactly an accent, in Calista's speech on occasion.

Xena, who was charming, and delighted the babe she carried was a boy.

The food was superb, and Natalya felt at ease… comfortable, she amended silently. Gigi began to tire, willingly retiring to bed for an overnight stay at her grandmother's home.

They were a pleasant family, Natalya perceived, extending polite interest in Natalya's role as Alexei's PA, her familiarity with the field of electronics... although not why, how or where she'd gained that knowledge.

It was after eleven when the evening drew to a close.

'You seem surprised,' Alexei drawled as the car cleared the drive and headed towards the inner city.

Perhaps because she'd expected...what? Cool reserve?

Why, when Alexei hadn't imagined it necessary to mention her existence in his life?

'In what way?' She could do cool, and tempered it with a touch of deliberate sweetness. 'Because you chose not to out me as my father's daughter?'

He shot her a quick glance before returning his attention to the traffic. 'Would you have preferred me to do so?'

'Perhaps I should thank you.'

'Give it up, Natalya.'

The atmosphere had taken a subtle change. A personal element that didn't sit well, for too many reasons she was reluctant to explore.

Consequently it was a relief when Alexei drew the car to a halt outside the hotel entrance, where a uniformed attendant hailed a waiting employee to drive the car down into the underground parking area.

A few words, a generous tip, and a leisurely pace

through the foyer to the bank of lifts…one of which swiftly transported them to their designated floor.

One day led to another, as Alexei, Cristos and Dimitri conducted high-powered meetings, each with their individual PAs in attendance, as they brokered deals, added valuable real estate to their company portfolio at a pace which left Natalya in awe of their combined expertise and staying power.

Ruthless power, she added silently, at the end of a particularly fraught day…one that was far from over. Debrief, dinner, highlight pertinent points from recordings, send same to Alexei's laptop. Shower, bed, sleep…

Except sleep proved elusive, and she lay staring sightlessly at the darkened ceiling for what seemed an age before emerging from the bed to pull on a wrap and quietly emerge into the lounge, where she crossed to the wide floor-to-ceiling glass sliding doors, parted the drapes a little and looked out over the brightly lit city, lingered on the kaleidoscope of neon signage on numerous city skyscrapers.

'It's a bit late to be admiring the view.'

Alexei's quiet drawl caused her breath to hitch as he moved to stand at her side.

'It beats counting sheep.' The words were out of her mouth before she gave them thought.

'Something is bothering you?'

You, she wanted to throw at him. *There, in my face… all day, every day. A constant I don't need or want.*

Because…she didn't want to explore the *why* of it.

Okay, she totally got the business part. What she hadn't bargained for was the constant twenty-four-seven away from home bit. Far away from where she could retreat at day's end to her own home. Dammit, her own sanctuary.

'Go to bed. We have another full day tomorrow.'

'Perhaps you should take your own advice.'

Admit he couldn't sleep? Her image haunted him, firing the need to pull her into his arms, claim her mouth with his own...and let whatever would happen, happen.

So why hesitate?

With any other woman he'd play the seduction game, accept the unspoken invitation and enjoy the sexual activity...heart untouched.

Natalya...their shared history was gaining too much intrusion on his original intention to gain revenge. So why now question what he'd believed to be fact?

Something didn't add up...but *what*?

He felt compelled to do the unexpected, and lifted a hand to trail light fingers down her cheek. And felt her tense.

'Don't.'

His mouth curved a little at the slight huskiness apparent in her voice. 'No?'

If she acted on sexual need, she'd tear the clothes from his body...and to hell with the consequences.

How many nights had she lain awake restless with the aching need of wanting him? *Only him.* Fighting an overwhelming urge to stem the tears that filled her eyes, angry with herself for lapsing into an emotional watershed as she wretchedly fought for control.

Alexei watched as she turned and escaped into her bedroom suite, heard the faint snap of the door clasp…and remained where he was for several long minutes, unaware of the night skyline, the many lit buildings, flashing multi-coloured neon, the traffic.

Instead he became caught up by her reaction… the faint quiver of her lips, the warmth of her cheek beneath his touch.

All too aware of his own body's damning response.

For the past five years he'd worked eighteen-to-twenty-hour days, fuelled by the need to succeed beyond measure in the name of revenge, ruthlessly crafting each move, each strategy in a personal vendetta where there could be only one survivor…*him*.

He'd won. Big time.

Satisfaction should be his…and it was.

So why this feeling a subtle shift had come into play?

The weekend provided a welcome change from the hectic week's business schedule. It was a beautiful day, and Natalya decided to revisit a few of the many glamorous stores and fashion boutiques New York city had to offer.

She was entitled to take some down time, to savour a coffee, a delicious pastry, browse a little…simply explore where the mood might take her. Sit a while, and watch the people walk by. Enjoy the cosmopolitan atmosphere.

Not to mention relax away from Alexei's powerful presence.

Something which earned a studied look from Alexei on learning her intention.

'Ensure you have your smartphone for contact, should it be necessary.'

It was simple to voice the few necessary words. 'Of course. Although I might remind you it's my day off.'

'But not the evening. The Delandros corporation sponsor an annual invitation-only dinner to commemorate my late father's love of his birthplace and Greek heritage. My mother insists you join us.'

Now there was the thing…an invitation from Calista Delandros made it difficult to refuse. 'I don't think it's…'

'Appropriate?' Alexei prompted.

'No.'

His smile held a tinge of amusement. 'Your reason being?'

'It's a significant occasion for family and friends. My position as your PA doesn't fit either category.'

'Consider it a personal request.'

'Personal is not on the agenda.'

A musing smile curved his mouth. 'The lines are becoming a little blurred.'

'Not,' Natalya confirmed, 'from my perspective.'

He wanted to change her mind, and would…soon.

Subtle persuasion was an art form, one he'd mastered at a young age. Only to realise seduction didn't equate to love, and while some women were content to play a part, he had tired of that game.

He wanted *more*.

'My mother will be disappointed if you refuse.' Manoeuvre and conquer was a skill in itself…one he owned unequivocally, and didn't hesitate to use to his advantage.

Natalya recognised it, wanted to call him on it, only to concede defeat. 'I accept, given the invitation came from your mother.'

The faint gleam of amusement momentarily apparent indicated he was one step ahead of her. 'I'll book a limousine for seven o'clock.'

'I'll ensure I'm on time.'

There was a sense of freedom as she rode the elevator to foyer level, declined the need for a limousine or taxi, and began to walk, choosing one of her favourite department stores in which to browse a while.

Coffee and a sinfully loaded pastry in a small café, followed by a gift for Ivana, a colourful top for Anja, a cute little doggy bow tie for Ben's pug Alfie.

It had proven to be a relaxing, enjoyable afternoon, and she entered the hotel suite ahead of time to discover it empty, a note in plain sight, which she quickly read before heading into her own suite.

A male could shower, dress and be ready in less time than a woman…

Nevertheless, Natalya was ahead of Alexei by five minutes, poised, attired in a tailored black skirt, matching camisole and a red silk box jacket. Stylish, flawless make-up, matching red lipstick, and diamond studs her only jewellery.

He did evening wear with superb masculine style.

Designer stubble added an edgy touch that set him apart, adding to an overall masculinity impossible to ignore.

'A drink before we leave?'

Natalya shook her head, and he checked his watch, caught up door swipe cards, then ushered her out of their suite.

The evening lay ahead…different from the usual social occasion, together with the pleasure of Calista and her family's company.

A limousine took them to a private venue in the city's outskirts where cars lined the streets, and the subdued beat of Greek music resonated in the evening air, softening as the four limousines carrying members of the Delandros family drew to a halt adjacent the main entrance of a large single-storey building.

'Smile,' Alexei bade quietly as the driver opened each door and ushered them to join Calista, followed by Cristos and Xena, then Dimitri.

The guests were greeted personally by each family member, which took a while, given a numbered ticket, until everyone was accounted for, seated…and the evening began.

An evening which was a mix of formality, anecdotes relayed in turn by Alexei, Cristos and Dimitri of a much-loved father. Reminiscences of times past, interspersed with the serving of food. Specialties of the region where Calista's husband was born. And laughter.

Truly a celebration of a life well-lived. Of honour, hard work, and the joy of family.

Later there was music, gentle, like the air drifting over the seas lapping the islands that made up Greece, the fishermen who dragged the nets, and the men, like Calista's husband, who had built many fine houses and villas on his beloved Santorini.

'Nothing like you expected?' Calista queried with a slow sweet smile as Natalya shook her head. 'We share this each year, and the money raised is gifted to those less fortunate. Soon there will be dancing, the music will become a little loud as the men move to the strains of the bouzouki. Each invitation carries a number for the prize of a ten-day cruise around the Greek Islands, including a three-day stay at a villa on Santorini.'

It was a beautiful sentiment, and Natalya said as much.

'My husband worked hard to provide our sons with a good education, to appreciate the good things in life, and to always remember where they came from.'

'Their success is a testament to you both,' Natalya offered with quiet sincerity.

'Thank you.'

The music proved enticing, and couples moved onto the dance floor, initially led by Alexei and his mother, followed by Cristos and Xena.

'Our turn,' Dimitri indicated, glimpsed her faint hesitation, and smiled. 'I don't bite.'

'Good to know.'

A younger version of Alexei, tall, well-built, easy-going with a sharp legal mind. Evidenced during the most recent meeting the three brothers had held with one of their competitors.

'Will you object if I pull you in a bit closer?'

She got it…or at least she thought she did. 'You're attempting to attract someone's attention?'

'Uh-huh.'

Natalya offered him a teasing smile. 'I doubt you'd fail attracting any young woman you chose to pursue. So you want me to appear as a decoy date,' Natalya teased. 'May I ask *who* has captured your attention? The gorgeous blonde eating you with her eyes? No? Hmm… The auburn-haired angel on the next table to our left, looking to kill you first chance she gets?' Given there was more than one titian-haired sophisticate in the room, Natalya added, 'The one wearing a stunning bronze-coloured gown, with a strand of diamonds showcasing a dazzling pendant showcasing her elegant décolletage?'

'You're more than just a pretty face,' Dimitri inclined with a faintly rueful smile, and she offered a light laugh.

'I'm trained to observe.'

His eyes assumed a musing gleam. 'Something you obviously do well.'

'Are you going to tell me who she is?'

'Curiosity, or genuine interest?'

'Interest,' Natalya answered quietly.

'A corporate lawyer in her father's firm.'

She smiled a little. 'Does she have a name?'

'If I told,' he enlightened as the edges of his mouth quirked a little, 'I would have to kill you.'

She wanted to laugh. 'Got it,' Natalya offered solemnly.

'So... Alexei?'

That came out of left field...and unexpected. Dimitri's eyebrow lifted a little. 'What's with the vibe between the two of you?'

'Your misinterpretation.'

His smile widened a little. 'I beg to differ.'

The music increased in beat, as almost everyone joined in with the laughter, and those couples dancing on the floor took a few missteps...which didn't appear to matter at all.

Voices rose, and Natalya gave a startled sound as Alexei appeared at her side and led her onto the dance floor before she had the opportunity to protest.

I don't know the steps, remained unsaid.

'It doesn't matter. I'll guide you.'

He did, and she soon mastered the rhythm, laughed a little when she almost missed a step, which Alexei faultlessly covered.

For the moment she simply let go, lost in the moment, the music, ambience...and the man who led her.

Until the moment the music slowed...and Alexei drew her close for timeless minutes, when it took all of her inner strength not to lean in against him, rest her cheek close to his heart, and just let the evening, the music, take her wherever it might lead.

Except there was an awareness of time and place, the haunting music, the slight pathos that seeped into her body, making her wish for more.

Did Alexei feel it too?

Who would know?

The sound of strings stirring from the bouzouki teased the air, and the chatter of conversation ceased as the pace lingered, dwelled, then began to quicken in tone and pitch. Stirring memories for most, of times past, and present for those who returned to revisit again and again in order to relive the magic merging of old and new, the history, the future.

Special, Natalya perceived, and felt the touch deep in her heart.

Coffee, thick, aromatic and strong, was served, after which the duplicate numbers handed out at the point of entry were presented in a circular glass tumbler, spun, and Calista, by tradition, extracted a ticket and read out the winning number.

There was a shout of victory, applause from the guests, the music lingered as the evening wound down, guests began making preparations to leave, with the sound of pleasurable laughter, affectionate farewells, car doors opening and closing, engines starting up as the streets slowly emptied.

It had been a memorable evening, and she said as much as she thanked Calista for the invitation, bade Xena, Cristos and Dimitri goodnight, before sliding into the limousine Alexei had summoned to return them to the hotel.

'You enjoyed the evening?'

Her mouth curved into a generous smile. 'It was great. The venue, the music. Uplifting to witness everyone coming together for a specific purpose. Reliving memories of times past, sharing lifelong friendships. Tradition,' she offered quietly.

Alexei shifted slightly to take in her vivacious features alight with pleasure, and held back the desire to pull her close, take her mouth with his own, and absorb her response.

There was a heaviness in his groin…needing, wanting what she could give him, as he would gift her. Sex, as a means to define love?

It didn't work that way. Love was a gift from the heart, inviolate, unconditional. A force of Nature shared by two people whose lives were inexplicably bound together for all time.

Hadn't he searched for its likeness in the intervening years? Only to despair a woman's interest was more attuned to his bank balance than his heart, his soul.

It hadn't been enough to put a ring on any woman's finger. Call him cynical, but he wanted *more* than a facsimile.

The limousine slowed and drew to a halt in the curved apex adjoining the hotel's main entrance. It was late, but the inner city remained alive with guests returning from drinks after the theatre, parties.

A city which never slept, Natalya acknowledged, as she rode the elevator to their designated floor.

The vibrant hype of the evening began to dissipate as she preceded Alexei into their suite, and she toed off her stilettos, discarded her jacket, and bade him goodnight.

He let her go.

And silently cursed…for lost opportunities.

Need...for a woman. Not just any woman...he could have any one of many who would give whatever he wanted. A wild eroticism among tangled sheets, each aware it was merely satiation of the senses, nothing more.

To his credit, he was selective...upfront, no false hope, mutual pleasure for as long as it lasted.

Sexual satisfaction for a price.

None of which applied to Natalya. For what they'd once shared rested deep within. A memory he'd failed to expunge...no matter what method he chose to apply.

She was *there*, as much a part of him as every breath he took...every beat of his heart.

Steely control...he possessed it in spades. In the boardroom.

Only a door separated him from Natalya's bedroom. He could breach it, seduce, and maybe succeed in gaining her compliance.

So why didn't he?

Damned if he knew.

Yet he did.

Aware losing wasn't an option.

CHAPTER THIRTEEN

THE FOLLOWING FEW days were business-oriented, with meetings between Alexei, Cristos and Dimitri as they explored strategies for a major takeover of a company on the brink of financial collapse.

Natalya's recordings were lengthy, the content involved as each man added input, opinions regarding the need for further investigation, relevant sources… calling a coffee break for a short debriefing session.

A relief from the intensity of the past few hours, Natalya accorded as she placed an order for coffee.

'Amalgamated will play ball,' Dimitri projected as they regrouped. 'They don't have any option.'

'Unless United undercut you,' Natalya offered, immediately aware of three pairs of male eyes refocussing their attention.

'An interesting observation,' Cristos declared. 'Your basis being?'

'They tend to sideline, then jump in just as a competitive deal is due to be struck.'

Alexei's eyes narrowed as he leaned back in his chair. 'They're not one of the major players.'

Dimitri leant forward. 'You have experience of their tactics?'

She inclined her head. 'They know how to play the game.'

'So do we,' Cristos answered, shooting Alexei a glance.

'A back-up plan alternative, and play our hand close to our chest?'

Good thinking, aware just how well United had tied her father's negotiations in knots two years ago, and left Roman red-faced, bluffing, and totally out of his league.

'Well, there you go,' Dimitri accorded softly. 'PA is a misnomer.'

'I imagine Natalya's observation skills saved Roman Montgomery's lack of attention in the field of negotiations.'

If her father had listened, she added silently. Unfortunately he rarely did.

Natalya indicated the carafe. 'More coffee?'

Each man declined, and she bore Alexei's scrutiny with equilibrium, caught the faintly speculative gleam, and gathered the carafe, cups onto the tray and moved it to the sideboard.

The meeting continued, the pace broken from time to time as Dimitri sought to lighten proposed strategy with a little levity.

Which he did very well, causing Natalya to smile at his efforts, laugh a little at one of his witty takes on one of New York's scions of industry, known for his slight pomposity.

It was light fun, momentary, although at one point she had to stifle her laughter…which earned Dimitri a searing glance from Alexei.

The afternoon wound up, with paperwork dispensed into briefcases, with Dimitri heading out as Alexei accompanied Cristos from the apartment.

'Natalya is a highly valued PA.'

Alexei directed his brother a non-committal glance. 'I agree.'

'She is also Roman Montgomery's daughter,' Cristos commented. 'And the young woman you were involved with during your Sydney sojourn.'

'Apropos of…?' Alexei queried. 'Besides being none of your business.'

'You chose not to elaborate why you returned to New York following your sojourn in Australia.'

'Missing home, family, was a logical reason.'

'More than that, unless I'm mistaken.' He waited a beat, then added, 'Dimitri flirted with her. You didn't like it.'

'Natalya is my PA.'

'Dimitri likes to play. We both know it's harmless. Yet you considered Dimitri's attention inappropriate.'

'Out of place during a business meeting.'

'Dimitri was bent on getting a reaction.' Cristos sent Alexei a musing look. 'That he succeeded proved… interesting.'

Alexei's dark glare was accompanied by a terse, 'Back off.'

Cristos lifted both hands in a gesture of silent compliance, offered a commiserative smile that required no words, then turned and headed towards the bank of elevators.

Natalya focussed on what she did best...encapsulating key points during the day's board meeting. Ensuring lunch reservations were in place, and displaying smooth efficiency as she dealt with unforeseen interruptions, while remaining cool, calm and collected.

Everything her position entailed and required.

By day's end, all she wanted to do was change, shower, slip into comfortable clothes...and chill.

Good luck with that, a tiny voice taunted, as a call came through stating the power brokers affiliated with the financially ruined company were ready to deal.

Chilling was out as she accompanied Alexei to the bank of elevators, one of which would deposit them to the floor housing several boardrooms where a take no prisoners negotiation took place, which the Delandros brothers won. A deal reluctantly struck, legalities approved, paperwork signed.

A coup to add to the Delandros portfolio.

Any form of celebration would be delayed until the legal formalities were complete.

Natalya glanced at the wall clock, made an attempt to shake off the weariness creeping through her body as she followed the men from the boardroom.

She was tired, it was late, she required time to destress, and importantly gain a few hours' sleep before rising soon after dawn to begin dealing with the follow-on from the evening's meeting. Right at that moment she silently acceded she earned every cent of her generous salary.

'Congratulations,' she offered as Alexei closed the door after they entered their suite, watching as he shrugged off his jacket and loosened his tie.

He spared her an intent glance, noted the shadows beneath her eyes, the tense edges of her mouth, the faint droop of her shoulders…and felt a degree of empathy for the long day, the even longer night.

Without a word he tossed his jacket onto a nearby chair, followed it with his tie, then he crossed to stand within touching distance, laid a hand on each shoulder, and began massaging the tight muscles, easing out the kinks, the tightness.

Natalya didn't move, couldn't…it felt so good, as he worked his magic easing the pain, and gradually the stress began to ebb…to be replaced by something… *more*, as he removed the clips from her hair and trailed light fingers over her scalp, soothing, taking her to a place where it would be so easy to succumb.

The touch of his lips to her forehead, lingering at her temple, the gentle whisper-like touch as he reached the edge of her mouth, savoured a little, then brushed the soft seam with a wicked promise of seduction.

A slow savouring persuasion, which left Natalya spellbound, uncaring where it might lead…only to baulk as reality began to descend.

She'd been down this road before, become pregnant and suffered a miscarriage. Hadn't the obstetrician advised in future certain steps should be taken prior to falling pregnant in order to avoid another miscarriage?

Birth control…she wasn't on any. Her mind spiralled…what if Alexei wasn't prepared? And even more alarming…what if she fell pregnant?

She closed her eyes, then slowly opened them again as a voice in her head silently screamed no.

'I don't do casual sex,' she managed carefully.

'I want you in my life,' Alexei said quietly.

She took care to meet his eyes, unsure what to say…or whether to say anything at all.

He lifted a finger and traced a gentle path over her lips. 'Is it too much to ask we share what we once had?'

She was willing to swear her heart took a downward flip. Lover? Mistress?

She closed her eyes, then slowly opened them again.

'I don't do the mistress thing,' she said carefully.

At that precise moment she hated herself for letting her guard down. Tempted, just once, to have him take her mouth with his own, to feel sensually alive. To accept whatever he offered, and to hell with the consequences.

She almost succumbed, knowing how easy it would be to lose herself…and that made her angry beyond measure.

Without thinking, she wrenched herself out of his arms, grabbed her jacket, the suite's swipe card and walked out of the door, uncaring of anything other than the need to get away from him, the hotel suite… to be *anywhere* but here.

Instead of summoning a lift, she chose the stairwell to the next floor down, made it to an elevator about to close, and took it down to street level.

The air was crisp, and she pulled the edges of her coat together as she exited the foyer.

The area was well lit, traffic moved quickly, and right at this moment she was too angry to consider the wisdom of walking alone late at night in a city not her own.

One block, crossing on to the second, becoming increasingly aware she should turn back.

Fool, she silently berated. What would this achieve?

Nothing. Other than reveal her lack of common sense.

One more block, then she'd turn and retrace her steps.

By which time her anger would have lessened, together with the dawning reality of place, time and the foolishness of walking alone on a New York street, prey to…whatever, whoever.

Enough.

Quickly followed by the realisation she'd left so quickly, she didn't have a bag, money…just the hotel swipe key.

Angry tears filled her eyes, and she brushed them away, turned…and witnessed Alexei closing the distance between them.

'You were *following* me?'

'A few metres behind you.'

'That's…' Words temporarily failed her as he moved in close and silenced her with a savage kiss, before easing into something else, gentling as his hands moved from her shoulders and slid down to cup her bottom, lifting her against his hard arousal, holding her there, his mouth softening to tease a little, then tangle her tongue with his own, sensuous, arousing, until she became lost to his persuasive touch, unaware her hands had crept unbidden to clutch his face, holding him close.

The sharp blast of a car horn, followed by a male catcall and a laughing voice demanding, *'Get a room!'* acted like a bucket of icy water, and Natalya released her hands and wrenched her mouth from his.

Her eyes changed from slumberous to startled fury as she began to struggle free…only to fail miserably.

'We're going to talk.' His eyes became dark ominous pools. 'Back at the hotel.'

Without warning he turned to face the opposite direction, holding her hand, pulling her along with him as he began walking, not even so much as flinching as she curled her fists and hammered his shoulderblades…anywhere she could reach with as much force as she could muster.

Alexei just kept walking.

She bore his silence for several long minutes, then she launched a punch into his ribcage…with no physical reaction whatsoever.

'Alexei, slow down,' she demanded. Causing a public scene had never been on her agenda…waiting a beat before adding, 'Please.'

'Will you behave?' His anger was quiet…too quiet. She drew in a deep breath, aware in a moment of clarity just how ridiculous it was to attempt to best him.

Temporary capitulation was the only option as she released her breath and briefly inclined her head. Relieved as he finally slowed down and released her hand.

There was wisdom in silence, and she refrained from uttering a further word until they reached their hotel. Together they crossed the marble-tiled foyer to the bank of elevators, all too aware the air between them could be cut with a knife.

Tall, dark, and silent, Alexei resembled a dangerous force as electronic doors opened, and two other couples followed them in.

Natalya deliberately looked straight ahead, ignoring him until the elevator reached their floor, choosing to walk ahead of him along the carpeted passageway to their suite, swiped the room card and she took three steps into the lounge before swinging round to face him.

'I want *out*.' Anger was a palpable entity she barely managed to control. She indicated the desk. 'My formal resignation will be there in the morning.' It provided a measure of satisfaction to turn her back and walk towards her suite.

Right at that moment she didn't give a *damn*.

She was *done*. With *him*, the situation she'd been manipulated into…all of it.

'I didn't figure you for a coward.'

Alexei's voice reached her as she was about to open the door to her suite, and she turned to spare him a scorching glare.

'Why? Because you kissed me?'

'You were with me every step of the way,' he offered quietly.

'I'm no longer the girl you once knew,' she retaliated.

'No?'

'You saw to that.'

His eyes darkened, sharpened. 'Enlighten me… how?'

'There's no point to this conversation.'

His entire stance stilled. 'I think there's every point.'

Natalya suddenly felt as if she was standing on the edge of a precipice, poised between the need to lash out in anger…or live to regret not imparting fact… as she knew it?

She tensed, every muscle in her body tightening as she recalled in minute detail the devastating discovery he'd disappeared out of her life.

'You left without a word. I called you. Many times. I made enquiries… *"The line has been disconnected."* I checked your apartment, hospitals, any and everyone I could think of who might have a clue to your whereabouts.' She tamped down the helplessness, and resorted to anger. 'I sent you texts. Emails. Desperately pleading for an answer. An explanation.'

She clenched each hand into a fist, felt her nails dig in each palm…and didn't even feel the painful sensation. '*Anyone* who could tell me whether you were alive or dead.'

The pain of him leaving her…even after five years, was still there…raw, aching, like a wound that had never truly healed.

Anger rose to the surface. 'Do you know what it's

like to wake each day…and hope *today* a call, text or email could ease the heartache? God willing in the best way possible? Only to fade into despair? Until eventually there's a need to accept whatever path you thought your life would take no longer existed?'

'Yes.'

She couldn't stop until she said it all. 'Worse, the agony of not knowing what went wrong? Why texts and emails remained unanswered?' She took a deep breath. 'To consider the worst scenario in each of many guises?'

He moved towards her and closed his hands over her shoulders. 'Back up a little,' he demanded quietly.

Her eyes blazed in anger. *'Why?'*

The ensuing silence became electric, and she closed her eyes in an effort to shut him out…only to have them widen as he took hold of her chin and tilted it.

She opened her mouth to berate him, except no word emerged as he pressed it closed.

'I didn't receive any texts or letters.'

She tore his hand away. 'You expect me to believe that?'

He stilled, his features hardening as a muscle clenched at the edge of his jaw. 'I left messages on your answering machine. Texts.' His eyes darkened. 'Are you saying they never reached you?'

The colour fled from her cheeks as uncertainty left her temporarily speechless. 'No,' she managed as her mind reeled. 'Nothing,' she said in a shocked whisper.

First and foremost, how it could have happened, followed seconds later by why?

She was reluctant to explore who, for it appeared highly unlikely anyone had access to her laptop, smartphone, snail mail.

Except…memory resurfaced in minute detail…her move to another apartment building, misplacing her smartphone, her father's decision to replace all their phones, both business and personal, with a different provider and new numbers. As well as a new email address for a reason that appeared valid at the time.

When?

Years ago. Her mind momentarily retraced the events back then, examined each sequence in detail, unaware of Alexei's narrowed scrutiny as he witnessed every fleeting emotion on her expressive features…and caught the moment she realised she had stepped into an unbelievable nightmare. Surely…it couldn't coincide…except it did.

Her father.

'How could he do such a thing?' Natalya's voice was an agonising whisper.

'Roman wanted you to marry up. I didn't come close to being a prospective candidate.'

'Tell me.' Her voice was calm…too calm. 'I need to hear what my father did. All of it.'

She deserved the truth…which he whittled down to essential detail. Leaving out his emotional turmoil, anger. Worse, the desperate need to discover *why*.

'Roman demanded I end my relationship with you, and presented me with a substantial cheque in a pay off. I tore it up.'

For the love of heaven. That her father would dare to go to such lengths to destroy their relationship was unconscionable. Unforgivable.

The disbelief, the silent anger.

The loss of *five years* of their lives.

Dear heaven, her miscarriage.

Natalya felt a cold hand clutch her stomach.

Sickened, almost literally, she briefly closed her eyes in an effort to retain a sense of calm. Opening them again, her eyes pierced his own, held steady, controlled...when inside she felt like screaming.

'He fired you, didn't he.' A statement, not a question. 'And threatened to make it impossible for you to get a position with any electronics firm in the country.' Her eyes locked with his own as she sought confirmation.

He didn't confirm or deny it...but then he didn't have to. The truth was there. Ugly, untenable, damning.

Did she realise how well he could read her? See the silent rage simmering beneath the surface?

She closed her eyes as Alexei reached for her and drew her close. There was magic in his touch, the way his lips sought the sensitive curve of her neck, savoured there, then he gently traced a path up to settle in the sweet hollow beneath her earlobe.

Evocative eroticism stirred something deep inside and spread through her body in sweet sorcery, dispensing with inhibitions and making her want so much more.

A faint groan emerged from her throat as he lifted and carried her into the bedroom.

He felt the warmth of her silent tears seep through his shirt, and brushed a kiss to the top of her head.

With care he slid her down his body to stand on her feet, and his gaze held her own as he carefully removed each item of clothing from her body.

She felt the warmth of his fingers as they trailed up her ribcage and unclipped her bra. Free, her breasts burgeoned in anticipation as he cupped each mound, and she bit back a gasp as his fingers sought the delicate peaks, traced them until they hardened beneath his touch.

Sensation arrowed deep inside, and she couldn't utter a word in protest as he lowered his head to one breast and took its peak into his mouth to lave it with his tongue.

Liquid fire coursed through her veins, heating her body to a point of madness.

Almost as if he knew, he lowered her evening trousers, traced a path up the inside of each thigh and sought the throbbing clitoris…brushing his fingers against the sensitive folds as she arched against him, unaware of the whispering plea emerging from her throat.

She was beyond sanity, filled with an aching need for his possession.

His clothes became an unwanted intrusion and were quickly discarded as they sought to touch, explore, as she became lost in the delight of tracing warm flesh, tight musculature, the sheer strength of his arousal.

She didn't want to wait. Wasn't aware of her soft

cries as he inserted a finger into the damp warmth between her thighs and skilfully brought her to orgasm, absorbing her guttural cry as she shattered.

It wasn't enough. She needed more, so much more, and he knew, teasing a little, taking time to lay his mouth against her own in a slow kiss that became sensual foreplay as she met and matched everything he gifted…then she gasped as he used a hand to pull aside the bed covers and lower her down onto the sheeted mattress.

She kissed him, teasing as he had teased her, and explored his body with light kisses, circling the tight masculine nipples, using her teeth to nip, the slide of her lips to soothe, before trailing to his navel, delicately laved it, before she turned her attention to the thick jutting arousal pulsing beneath her touch as she stroked its length with her tongue, reacquainting herself with its shape and throbbing size…heard his husky groan, and delighted in his throaty *you're killing me* an instant before firm hands took hold of her hips and eased her onto her back, holding her hands fast above her head as he trailed a path down the quivering flesh of her stomach. Lower, and she cried out as he suckled the damp flesh, nipped the sensitive folds with care, then used his tongue to send her mindless.

Her entire body felt as if it were on fire, and she gasped as he shifted over her and drove in deep, held still as she absorbed him, then he gently rocked, lengthening his thrusts until she reached the edge and came, as he did in unison, and there was only the euphoric ecstasy of two lovers in perfect accord…

mind, body, heart and soul as they gave everything there was to gift…before easing down to the sweet exhaustion of sexual fulfilment.

'*Amazing,*' Natalya whispered, and felt his lips drift gently over her skin, soothing her rapid pulse-beats, before exploring her lips, caressing with such tenderness she fought to hold back tears.

Lost, so completely *lost* in him, there was no sense of time or place. Only the need to cling to the pulsing thrum deep inside her body, and exult in sexual nirvana.

The musky scent of sensual heat combined with the dawning knowledge they'd just shared unprotected sex…

Dear heaven, what had she done?

They, she corrected silently. There were two of them in this bed, two who had seduced, shared, and exulted in their mutual passion.

Alexei caught each fleeting expression as the reality widened her eyes, the brief few startled seconds as her eyelids shuttered closed, only to open again as instinct kicked in together with a sense of *déjà vu*. Unfounded, according to rapid silent calculation.

She pushed at him, endeavouring to escape without success as he caged her in, his eyes dark as the blackest slate as he took in her expression.

Without a word Alexei rolled off the bed, scooped Natalya into his arms and walked into the en suite bathroom, turned on the shower and carried her beneath the pulsing water, collected the liquid soap, and began smoothing the lightly scented fragrance over her body in a slow sensuous slide that drove her wild… wanting, *needing* to respond in kind. His mouth curved into a sensual smile. 'Patience. You'll have your turn.'

She did. Eventually. Only it took a while. And later, towelled dry, he took her to bed, drew her close in against him.

She couldn't find the words—not the right ones. The extent of Roman's intervention devastated her, and merely confirmed the extent her father was prepared to go to in order to rule not only his company, but his family.

'There's something you should know,' Natalya said quietly. At the time she'd borne the heartache in the light of day, and let the tears fall during the dark of night when she was alone. Until there were no more tears to shed, and she gathered the resolve to get on with her life.

'I discovered I was pregnant.' She faltered in an effort to find the right words, and her mouth trembled as his hands shaped her face. His eyes were dark, silently questioning, and she couldn't look away.

'Why didn't you tell me?'

Her features paled, her eyes dark with an edge of pain, and he swore softly beneath his breath.

'I drove to your apartment after work.'

A lump rose in her throat, momentarily preventing speech, and she swallowed compulsively in an effort to allow her voice to emerge. 'You weren't there.' The words tumbled out. 'I rang your phone. No answer.'

Alexei stilled, his eyes almost black. 'When did you ring?' His voice was hard, urgent. 'What time?'

'Is time so important?'

'Yes.' He bunched his hands into fists. 'Dammit.' Yet he already knew. 'Think…please,' he added in a strained voice.

'After six…maybe six-thirty.'

He closed his eyes briefly in silent anguish at the hand of Fate. Ten…fifteen minutes after the police had taken him from his apartment, arrested by the hand of her father. His phone confiscated.

Theos.' The soft imprecation left his lips with the realisation she'd had to cope without his knowledge, or the benefit of his support.

Silent anger consumed him, together with the imminent need to take Roman Montgomery apart with his bare hands.

Her words hurt like a stab to the heart as memory surfaced in vivid Technicolor detail.

The anger…helpless rage at Roman Montgomery's manipulative machinations.

Natalya felt his lips rest against her forehead, then trail gently down her cheek to rest at the edge of her mouth, soothing the trembling seam as he held her close.

Roman, Natalya determined fiercely, was about to be called to account. She'd call and invite him to share lunch with her, then calmly…surely she could *do* calm several hours from now?

'He's going to pay.'

'Natalya,' Alexei cautioned, and she shook her head.

'You don't understand.'

But he did. All too well. The silent rage that had

almost destroyed him, the desire to succeed beyond measure.

Not the least of it, to throw that success in Roman's face. As he had with deliberate intent, using his business nous to prove he could. Then plotted his revenge against the man who'd wielded God-like power…using Natalya as a weapon.

Ill-founded, as he discovered…and beat down the rage simmering beneath the surface.

How could a father do that to his own daughter?

As easily as Roman succeeded in deceiving his own wife. A self-absorbed narcissist who put his own needs first and foremost…without exception.

Alexei wanted to slam a fist against something… for a few brief seconds he almost did. Just for the hell of it.

Almost as if she knew, she lifted a hand to his cheek.

'Natalya…'

Her eyes seared his own, steady, obdurate. 'There's nothing you can say to stop me confronting my father.'

He waited a beat, then offered quietly, 'Think it through,' he advised gently, and watched her eyes narrow.

'He doesn't deserve consideration.'

CHAPTER FOURTEEN

THERE WAS A need for planned strategy. An assemblage of irrefutable facts. Cool, sans anger. Absence of a public scene.

In Roman's true sense of style, he'd vetoed a small restaurant in favour of one of his favoured upmarket haunts noted for its fine cuisine.

Natalya entered the boutique restaurant several minutes past the appointed time, for, in truth, she wanted her father to be seated and waiting.

It helped that he was there, charming the wait staff in his typical style. The smile, a flirting tease in his eyes...just enough not to offend, but holding a silent invitation, should it be accepted.

Natalya touched a hand to Roman's shoulder to catch his attention, and he turned at once, offering a warm greeting as he caught her hand and lifted it to his lips.

'Darling girl.' Ever the showman, he gave the waitress a knowing smile. 'Better late than never.'

Did he ever stop? And to think she'd always put his teasing down to his consummate charm.

'Have the sommelier choose the finest champagne

and have it brought to the table,' he instructed the waitress in a grandiose manner, 'A celebration.'

He might think otherwise by the time their meal concluded.

'Problem with traffic?' Roman enquired as Natalya slid into the chair opposite.

'Parking,' Natalya enlightened, and when the champagne was presented, checked, approved and opened she instructed, 'Just a small amount. I have to work this afternoon.'

She waited, sipped superb champagne and exchanged small-talk as she selected an entree, refused a main, and settled for a lemon sorbet to follow.

The waitress served coffee, and Natalya added milk, sat back and mentally directed...*now.*

She kept it brief, citing irrefutable fact with admirable restraint...and took some satisfaction as her father stiffened, blustered a little, then paled as she relayed knowledge of each pertinent detail...the co-incidence of her lost smartphone and its replacement with a different provider and new number.

Coinciding with Alexei's disappearance from her life.

'Don't,' she cautioned as he attempted to speak, 'attempt to justify your actions. Your manipulative meddling was unforgivable.'

'I wanted the best for you.'

She battled with anger, and fought to contain it.

'Without thought for my right to choose?'

'Delandros had nothing. He could never have supported you in the style you deserved.'

Leave now, a silent voice urged…before you say something regrettable.

Natalya rose to her feet, caught up her bag and walked to the cashier's desk, produced a credit card, paid the bill, then she emerged onto the sidewalk, covered the three blocks to where she'd parked her car.

Alexei was at the industrial plant, the rest of the afternoon was hers, and there was a need to occupy her mind and minimise any inclination to dwell on her father's actions.

She aimed the car remote, then slid in behind the wheel, had a flash of inspiration and delved into her bag for her smartphone. Minutes later she engaged the engine, eased out of the parking bay and headed towards fashionable Double Bay.

A relaxing facial, some one-on-one time with Anja…what could be better?

'Thanks for fitting me in,' Natalya greeted with affection as she took her place in one of the beauty rooms.

Bliss, absolute bliss to simply close her eyes and let every muscle in her body slowly relax as Anja worked her magic.

'Are you going to update me? Over the past few days a number of regular clients have quizzed me if the rumours are true about you and Alexei.'

'Which you refrained from providing.' It was a statement of fact.

'You know better.'

Yes, she did. They'd shared much over the years, and maintained a mutual trust.

Yet she hesitated…the sex with Alexei was great. Okay, *fantastic*. The question being what their future might hold. Or if they had a future.

There were words left unsaid, and while she ached for the whole package…did Alexei want the same? Or would it be her fate to remain his PA with benefits?

'Hello?' Anja prompted. 'Natalya to Planet Earth?'

'There are issues,' Natalya admitted, and glimpsed Anja's faintly wry smile.

'Resolve them. Anything less is a cop-out.'

'What would you suggest?' Natalya queried, *sotto voce*. 'Grab Alexei by the scruff of his neck, pin him to the floor, and demand his intentions?'

'That would be my modus operandi.'

Natalya bit back a light laugh. 'I'll remind you of that when the love bug strikes.'

'Not going to happen anytime soon.'

'Famous last words.'

'Keep your eyes closed,' Anja ordered. 'I'm not done yet.' Firm hands created their own magic, and Natalya uttered a pleasurable sigh. 'Something you're not telling me?'

'Nothing to tell.'

Not yet, Natalya perceived. She could wait, and would, aware there was a time and a place, and now wasn't it.

Natalya's phone chirped with an incoming text as she entered her home.

Dinner tonight. I'll collect you at six. Alexei.

She checked her watch, saw there was ample time in which to change, and then took a leisurely shower, towelled dry, stepped into her bedroom, and riffled through the contents of her wardrobe. Formal or semi-formal?

The latter appeared a safe choice, and she selected a stylishly cut dress in emerald-green.

Ear studs, a simple necklace, black heels, a black clutch with essentials, then she caught up a black wrap and she was good to go within minutes before the appointed time. On cue the security gate buzzer sounded and she crossed to the video link, identified Alexei and released the locking mechanism.

He was waiting for her as she opened the front door, attired in casual trousers, open-necked shirt and casual jacket. Tall, ruggedly attractive… Her stomach flipped as heat flooded her body as she walked into his outstretched arms, lifted her face for his kiss and breathed him in, relishing the moment as his arms pulled her close.

Nice. She could have stayed longer…resisting the urge to invite him in, suggest they forgo dinner, and eat later. Much later.

Except he trailed his mouth to the sweet curve of her neck, savoured briefly, then took hold of her hands linked behind his neck and brought one to his lips.

'Food,' Alexei opined with a wicked smile, and led her to the sleek Aston Martin waiting kerbside.

Natalya wondered which restaurant Alexei had chosen as he eased the luxury car into traffic. A boutique place in one of the suburbs, or city venue.

Not a restaurant, she discovered as the car headed towards one of the elite northern suburbs where residences commanded multimillion-dollar prices, and were guarded by high-tech security.

Alexei turned into a tree-lined street and slowed the car before a wide set of high black elaborately scrolled gates, beyond which stood a graceful two-level residence at the apex of a semi-circular driveway.

Were they dining as guests at a private home?

His home, appeared the correct answer, as he used a remote to open the gates and eased the car towards the front entrance.

Immaculate lawns bearing some decorative sculpted shrubbery, and there were borders bearing a beautiful array of flowers lining the driveway.

The front door opened as he disengaged the engine, and a middle-aged woman stood waiting to welcome them.

'My housekeeper, Lisette,' Alexei informed her quietly as he curved an arm across Natalya's shoulders and drew her forward, effecting introductions.

Together they entered a large circular foyer with a marble-tiled floor, showcasing a sweeping double staircase leading to an upper level.

Lisette greeted Natalya with a pleasant smile before turning towards Alexei. 'I expect you would enjoy a drink in the lounge. Dinner will be served at seven in the private dining room.'

'Thanks, Lisette.'

He turned towards one of four heavily panelled doors leading off from the lobby and led her into a spacious lounge, closed the door behind them, then pulled her close.

What began as a gentle kiss soon became an evocative tasting as he explored her mouth, and she met and matched him, luxuriating in his touch as she lifted her arms to link each hand at his nape.

Natalya's entire body came alive, as the kiss moved up a few levels, where the urge to dispense with his clothes…and have him remove her own, became almost impossible to ignore.

She wanted to slide the palms of her hands over his naked skin. Explore the tight muscles sculpting his body, admire the strength apparent, and savour every inch with her mouth as she drove him wild.

Then welcome him into her body as they became lost in each other…lust, avid, earthy and beyond mere words.

Love, as it had been in what seemed to be another lifetime when they had implicit trust in each other.

Alexei gently shifted his hands to cup her face. He traced her cheek with his thumb, his eyes dark as he examined her features.

'I'll get you a drink.'

Did she look as if she needed one? Probably. 'Preferably non-alcoholic.' It was a while since lunch, and she recalled she'd eaten very little. 'I'll have some wine with dinner.'

Alexei moved to the drinks cabinet, retrieved two crystal wine glasses, filled one with mineral water, the other with white wine, then he retraced his steps and placed a glass in her hand.

She avoided the prosaic, and went for the most relevant.

'I had lunch with my father today.'

His eyes sharpened. 'He upset you?'

'In hindsight…not so much.' Surprising, given how much pain Roman's actions had caused her. 'I said what I wanted to say, paid the bill, and walked out of the restaurant.'

She possessed an inner strength. Yet he sensed the hurt, her loss of trust for her father's almost criminal meddling. Worse, perhaps, for having been totally unaware of her father's other life.

Roman had created the perfect cover in choosing Natalya as his PA.

Which bore the question of Ivana's wealth and social standing…somehow it didn't add up with the woman he'd come to know. Her values, her unconditional love for her daughter.

Perhaps a woman was entitled to her reasons, none of which were his to attempt to explore.

Of one thing he was certain. Natalya's total loyalty to her mother.

'You have a beautiful home,' Natalya complimented as they entered a tastefully furnished dining room.

'Which I will show you after dinner,' Alexei said as he led her to the table and withdrew her chair.

The housekeeper had excelled herself, providing a seafood entree, followed by perfectly grilled salmon steaks accompanied by a delicious salad, with fresh fruit compote for dessert.

Later they took coffee on the terrace, relaxed following a pleasant meal. The view over the harbour to the city with its buildings lit and rising high against a darkened sky presented a superb panorama. Coloured neon signage promoting varying products, the moving headlights of passing traffic…mere pinpricks observed from this distance.

Peaceful, tranquil. A place that could be a home, filled with love, perhaps children…

A vision of which the stuff of dreams was made. Not always the reality.

So where did they go from here?

The word love hadn't been mentioned.

Alexei unwound his length from the chair, leant forward to take hold of her hands and gently pulled her to her feet and into his arms.

His touch, the brief flare of unguarded emotion in his eyes…dear heaven, his kiss…sensuality at its peak as his tongue curled around her own, tasted, teased, gentling a little at the sound of her despairing groan as he went in deep, persuasive, pervading as he gifted his heart…his soul.

It was more, so much more than she believed possible, and seemingly an age before he lifted his head, his eyes dark as he glimpsed her flushed cheeks, the soft mouth slightly swollen from his touch, and caught the faint quiver as she visibly sought control.

He lifted a hand to smooth the pad of his thumb over the fullness of her lower lip. 'Stay with me tonight.'

Her eyes lit with a tinge of humour. 'Presumably this isn't a work-related request?'

'Not even close.'

'I'll give it some thought,' she said, delighting in teasing him.

Without a word he led her inside, secured the terrace doors, set the security alarm, moved towards the beautifully curved staircase leading to an upper floor and the master bedroom.

He took it slow and easy, removing each item of her clothing, as she unbuttoned his shirt and slipped it from his body. Loving the muscular chest, the tight abs, the strength apparent in his broad shoulders.

'Don't stop.'

Natalya reached for the belt at his waist. 'Just savouring the moment.'

'Uh-huh. You want some help there?'

She traced the bulging length of his arousal pressing against the zip, and offered him a witching smile. 'Got it covered.'

'Uncovered is better.'

'No foreplay?'

'As much as you can take.'

'That sounds interesting.'

Interesting didn't equate to what they shared as he slowly removed each item of her clothing, pausing to press his lips to each pulse, his hands intent on shaping every curve until she trembled, on fire, wanting, *needing* him inside her...so much, she was unaware of the faint sounds slipping unbidden from her throat, the way her hands moved on him…and her satisfaction as he took her mouth with his own in a kiss that sent her over the edge.

'You want to hear there has been no one who mattered since you?' Alexei queried quietly.

In one easy movement he leant forward and stripped the covers from the large bed, then he laid her down on the cool sheets and moved over her body.

Now…or she'd have to beg.

And then she did, as he trailed his lips down her stomach to the moist heat below, using his mouth, his tongue, to drive her wild.

Then he positioned himself and drove in hard, exulting in the feel of her, the way her inner muscles contracted around his length when he began to move, slowly at first, building sensation to an exhilarating peak, held them both there as an intense orgasm took them high, consuming mind, body and soul.

So excruciatingly sensual she had no memory of crying out in ecstasy…nor was she aware of his own groan of release as they lay joined together, too caught up in the deliciously slow ebb of exquisite pleasure.

Natalya didn't want to move…wasn't sure she could, until the wonderful lethargy consuming her body settled a little.

It felt good, so incredibly *right* to snuggle her cheek into the curve of his neck, to bury her lips into the hollow and savour his musky heat, feel the strong beat of his heart as he tethered her close.

Later, so much later, Alexei gathered her up into

his arms and headed to the en suite bathroom, set the
shower into action, and held her beneath the pulsing
warm water as he smoothed liquid soap over every
inch of her body with such evocative slowness it was
nothing less than seduction.

With a witching smile Natalya took the container
of liquid soap from his hand, moved to stand behind
him, cupped a handful of soap and administered slow
sweeping strokes across his shoulders, down his back,
covering the taut slopes of his buttocks, then turned
him round to face her.

She could do evocative slowness as well as he
did, and his eyes became dark, faintly hooded, as
she teased a little, plucking lightly at his nipples, felt
them tighten beneath her touch, then she moved to
his shoulders, his arms before trailing down his ribcage to settle a hand on each hip.

'If you stop there,' he declared with a throaty
drawl, 'you will suffer.'

'I'm afraid,' she mocked quietly, and offered him
a mischievous grin as he caught hold of her shoulders. 'Very afraid.'

'Witch,' Alexei accorded with dangerous softness
as he lowered his head and took her mouth in a passionate kiss that robbed her of breath.

At the same time his hands slid down her back,
cupped her bottom and lifted her high against him,
caressed the softness of one breast, then sought her
burgeoning nipple, tasted, teased, before drawing it
into his mouth.

Intense sensation spread through her body, co-alescing at the most sensitive part of her femininity, and she gasped as he trailed a hand over her stomach, palming the indentation as his mouth moved to render a similar salutation to her other breast, where he took her almost to the edge as he teased, tasted and lightly caught the nipple with the edge of his teeth.

Heat rose deep within, and she gasped as his hand trailed low…way too low as he sought the sensitive folds protecting her clitoris.

Her mouth parted with a soft gasp as he stroked the delicate bud until she almost reached begging point.

He slid a finger into the moist passage, heard her unbidden groan and felt the restless movement of her legs, aware she needed more…*more* than this slow delicate, exploratory, teasingly intimate foreplay.

Natalya curled her fingers around his thick arousal, squeezed a little, and sensed Alexei's quick intake of breath.

In one easy movement he carried her into the bedroom, tossed back the covers, then he sought her mouth with his own, staking a claim that seared every erogenous pulse in her body as he brought her to tumultuous orgasm, stilled a little, then he began to move, slowly at first, then with deeper intensity, driving them both towards a mutual orgasm that left her temporarily bereft of the ability to breathe. Sensual overload…and then some.

There were no words, just a whisper of a heartfelt sigh escaping from her lips.

She didn't want to move…didn't think she could as Alexei held her close for what seemed an age, until sleep overcame them both.

Only to wake in the early morning hours to the touch of his mouth against her own as he made love to her with such exquisite gentleness she wanted to weep. Lazy pre-dawn sex, infinitely sensual, Natalya managed as Alexei curved her close to his muscular frame. Exquisite and a beautiful beginning to a new day.

'Sleep,' he murmured as he pulled up the bedcovers.

The next morning, showered, dressed, they shared a wholesome breakfast together on the terrace, took a refill of coffee, after which Alexei drove her home, settled his mouth on her own, then headed into the city.

There was time to feed Ollie, exchange her clothes for office wear, a slimline skirt, silk blouse, jacket, make-up, check her satchel and head into the city.

A day where *work* took priority, which was a blessing, for it allowed Natalya little or no time to think… or in her case, over-think.

Alexei slipped easily into professional mode, moving it up a notch as he liaised with Marc Adamson, chaired an intense meeting, took a business lunch which ran over time and by day's end she required every ounce of energy in order to match Alexei's pace…while he appeared as if he'd enjoyed a good night's sleep instead of a mere few hours.

In truth, she was in a state of ambivalence. Unsure of what their future held.

* * *

One day led to another, each following a familiar pattern as Natalya dealt with everything Alexei threw at her.

While the nights were something else…spent at his mansion, her apartment. Emotive, passionate.

Until one evening when Alexei offered the words she longed to hear.

'Marry me.'

Not I love you…can't live without you.

'I want you in my life.'

Want, not need. 'In your bed,' she managed evenly, and saw his eyes narrow slightly as she slid out of his bed and began pulling on her clothes in the moonlight streaming in from the night sky.

'That, too.'

It took all her resolve to utter the one word she'd hoped never to have to say to him. 'No.'

His expression remained unchanged. 'Marriage is not important to you?'

Yes. Just not merely another merger added to your life portfolio.

'I'm content with my life the way it is.'

'What if I want more?'

Five years ago she'd believed their love was inviolate, a permanent entity that would entwine their lives for a lifetime.

'Qualify "more".'

Your heart, gifted unconditionally. Words she couldn't, wouldn't voice.

She needed her own space, her own bed. Without

a word she gathered up her bag, her keys, bade him a polite goodnight…and left. Waiting until she used the remote to close the gates guarding Alexei's residence.

Fool, she silently chided as she traversed the streets towards her home.

CHAPTER FIFTEEN

NOT THE DESIRED result Alexei had envisaged.

Five years of hard business negotiations had resulted in paring details down to the bare essentials... cut-throat minimalist facts.

Successful in the business arena.

A complete failure when it came to proposing marriage.

He wanted to hit something, and almost did...except doing so wouldn't achieve the desired result.

There was a flashback to the night he'd intended to ask Natalya to share his life.

The champagne on ice. Flowers...her favourite roses, tastefully assembled in clear cellophane with a note expressing his love. The for ever, until death do us part in poetic prose. The ring, the delicate diamond, the best he could afford at the time, put on hold and paid off in increments from his fortnightly wage. Her favourite food.

The evening she didn't arrive.

Her smartphone cut off.

Alexei's arrest.

History.

Which had no part in the *present*…or the future.

He picked up the phone, punched in numbers, made a few calls, cancelled two appointments, and set the next day in motion.

A day in which Alexei spent time with Marc Adamson caught up in meetings with Marc's PA in attendance. Not entirely unusual, Natalya perceived…nor was the late afternoon text requesting her presence at a restaurant on the other side of the city.

Despite the location not being one she perceived Alexei would normally choose. Who was she to judge? Presumably privacy was key, with no intrusion from the media.

Parking wasn't difficult, and she slid in behind Alexei's Aston Martin…a surprise, given his preference for the limousine with Paul at the wheel.

Whatever…it hardly mattered. She was here in her capacity as Alexei's PA, with no time to delay if punctuality was key.

She walked through the door, and paused, initially puzzled at the lack of patrons. There was only one occupant… Alexei, who rose to his feet as she crossed to his side.

'Has there been a delay?' She glanced up as a waiter appeared out of nowhere and pulled out a chair for her. 'I take it your guests are late?'

'No guests,' Alexei said quietly as he placed a hand to the back of her waist. 'Please, sit down.'

She sank into the chair and a faint frown creased her forehead. 'There's no meeting?'

'Not tonight.'

'Then why are we here?'

It was difficult to read his expression, and her eyes widened as the lights brightened a little, and another waiter appeared bearing an ice bucket holding a bottle of champagne.

For a brief second she thought she got it…only to dismiss the possibility as a flight of fancy. Until the waiter popped the cork and poured a measure of champagne for Alexei to savour and approve…a mere formality, given the exclusive label…before carefully pouring a quantity of the sparkling liquid into two crystal flutes.

Alexei lifted his flute, touched its rim to her own, and gently named the toast… 'To us.'

Natalya's lips parted, but no words emerged.

Light muted music wafted from hidden speakers, and a waitress appeared with a silver platter, on which lay a single red rose and a personalised card.

Natalya simply looked at him as he removed both and placed them in front of her.

'I planned a surprise evening five years ago… champagne, food,' he revealed quietly. 'A ring to seal our love.'

Her lips quivered a little, and there was nothing she could do to prevent the single tear escaping to slowly trickle down one cheek.

He leant forward and carefully brushed it away. 'I love you. For the beautiful woman you are, in heart, mind and spirit.'

Her heart stopped beating, then quickened a little

as she attempted to say the words caught in her throat, only to feel the press of his finger against her lips.

'Last night…'

Natalya's eyes softened as she resisted the temptation to interrupt him. Was it asking too much to want to hear the words?

'Will you marry me? Please.'

It was the *please* that did it for her. 'Yes.'

He rose to his feet and caught her close, his mouth on hers as she clung to him. Unaware of time or place…until he gently released her, and the restaurant, the importance of the evening returned to focus.

'There are words,' she offered quietly, 'written, said, for momentous occasions such as this. Poetic prose escapes me…you're my only love. *Yours*, for as long as I draw breath.'

Alexei's eyes darkened with slumberous passion. 'I'll hold you to that.'

It was her turn to tease him a little. 'I'd hoped you might.'

He drew her apart a little and reached into his pocket, withdrew a ring, took hold of her left hand and slid a magnificent solitaire diamond onto her finger.

For a breathtaking few seconds, she couldn't find the words. 'It's beautiful,' Natalya accorded with quiet reverence. *Stunning*, she added silently. A visual testament to his wealth and power.

'But?'

'The ring you bought five years ago,' she began. 'Do you still have it?

'Why do you ask?'

The thought he might have kept it held such meaning. Bought with an emotion-filled heart…a symbol of everlasting hope, love, and the intention of them spending their lives together.

The ring he'd placed onto the third finger of her left hand flashed brilliant fire as caught by the steady flickering candle. Magnificent and ruinously expensive.

'It represents the love we shared at that time.'

'And that is important to you?'

There were words she could say, a few of which she had already expressed. 'Yes.'

A warm smile curved his lips. 'Are you going to tell me why?' A diamond worth little in comparison to the ring which now replaced it.

Natalya lifted both hands to frame his face, her expression soft with emotion, and incredibly beautiful. 'You need to ask?'

No, he didn't.

'Will you mind if I accept this ring as a commitment gift representing everlasting love throughout all the years we'll share together, and wear it on the third finger of my right hand?'

Alexei shook his head and offered a quizzical smile. 'And the original ring?' he teased.

'Suspended on a gold chain close to my heart.'

She was something else. 'If it pleases you.'

'Thank you.'

He gave a soft laugh. 'I'll commission the jeweller

to craft a wide wedding band.' Encrusted with diamonds, he added silently.

He knew her so well, her values, ideals…her generous loving heart.

His for ever…all the days and nights of his life.

She reached up and kissed him. 'Perfect.'

So too was the evening.

The champagne, the food, ambience…a special memory that was theirs alone.

One, Alexei determined, they would celebrate each year for the rest of their lives.

The next thing on their agenda was to inform Natalya's parents before the ring on her finger resulted in a media article citing rumour and supposition. Even if the ring didn't appear on her left hand, the mere sight of it would draw comment, assumptions would be made… and Ivana deserved better than to hear such important news second-hand.

It was okay to be cool-headed in all things business…inviting her parents to dinner to formally announce an engagement, followed by a wedding, was something else.

Alexei and Roman in the same home, the same room? 'You're stressing too much,' Alexei chastised gently. 'Ivana will be delighted.'

'Perhaps I should pre-warn her?'

'In order for her to pre-warn your father?'

He read her too well. 'Something like that.'

Alexei touched a light finger to her cheek. 'I'm sure Roman will be the consummate guest.'

If not, he'd deal with it.

Natalya planned the menu with care, choosing each course with her parents in mind. Cuisine was one of her skills, and she made lists, selected the best ingredients, took care with the dining room setting, using the finest linen inherited from her *babushka*, a favoured dinner set, fine crystal, and silverware. Faintly scented candles.

A double-check, a change of clothes to pencil-slim linen skirt with matching silk top, make-up, hair… done.

'What do you think?'

Alexei crossed to her side and laid his mouth to the sweet hollow at the edge of her neck. 'Amazing.'

He was her rock, the love of her life…everything.

Designer black trousers, a pristine white shirt unbuttoned at the neck, the shadowed designer stubble… eyes so expressively dark as he smiled.

Hers. Truly hers…as she was his.

Together again, as they were meant to be.

Not by luck…*faith.*

'It's perfect,' he accorded quietly. 'So, too, are you.'

'Don't make me cry, or I'll have to…' she caught the musing gleam in his dark eyes '…go fix my make-up, and leave you to greet the parents.'

'For a moment I thought you might be considering an interesting diversion.'

She trailed light fingers down his cheek, the soft designer stubble to the edge of his mouth. 'Later.'

'I'll hold you to that.' He lowered his lips to her forehead. 'You're my love, my life.'

'Same goes.'

At that moment the external buzzer sounded, and she watched as Alexei crossed to release the gate mechanism.

There were hugs, a mutual handshake between Alexei and Roman, who expressed his appreciation for the invitation, while Alexei attended to serving drinks in the lounge.

Ivana's delight, her appreciation of Natalya's ring.

Warm, friendly…even Roman appeared to behave himself, and it became easy to relax a little.

Fine wine preceded the starter, followed by the main course, eaten in a leisurely fashion. Conversation flowed, as Roman made an effort to engage, sans his usual bonhomie. Dessert was a pavlova variation created by Natalya's grandmother…crisp meringue, soft on the inside, covered with whipped cream and drenched in fruit and their juices.

'Perfection, darling,' Ivana complimented, adding to Natalya's pleasure, 'Let me help you in the kitchen while Roman enjoys his customary after-dinner cigar.'

A familiar ritual following a lifetime of family lunches and dinners for as long as Natalya could recall.

Alexei stood to his feet. 'I'll join you.'

This evening's short sojourn would hopefully create an emerging bond of sorts between Alexei and her father. Each had issues to be resolved, and although the timing wasn't perfect…at least it might help both men to move forward.

Natalya waited until the men had moved out on the back terrace, and spared her mother a quick glance, received a reassuring smile. 'I'll be okay.'

Alexei closed the door quietly and indicated the decorative gazebo at one end of the terrace, waited until they reached it, and they stood facing each other while Roman extracted a cigar, expertly clipped the end, then his lighter flared, and he took the first draw.

Alexei kept it brief, merely the bare facts, and lowered his voice.

'Five years ago you went to extraordinary lengths to separate me from Natalya. You deleted text messages from Natalya's cell phone, wiped her answering machine clean and misappropriated her mail. Information I imagine you'd prefer to remain buried?'

'Are you threatening me?'

'Not at all. Merely assuming you'll want to attend your daughter's wedding and share a part in your future grandchildren's lives?'

Roman closed his eyes, then slowly opened them again and inclined his head. 'Yes.'

'Then we understand each other.' Alexei extended his hand, which Roman shook, then Alexei indicated the nightscape, the sprinkling of electric lamplight in the distance, the moving vehicles along major traffic roads, and the darkness of the ocean beyond. 'An attractive view, by day or night.'

'Yes. The home which once belonged to Ivana's mother.'

'So I understand.'

'A hardworking feisty lady,' Roman imparted. 'Who spoke her mind.'

'Of whom Natalya was very fond,' Alexei reminded, which drew a nod in silent agreement.

'Shall we return indoors? Share champagne, raise a toast to the future…and family.'

In hindsight the evening proved a pleasant one, as Ivana suggested lunch to initiate pre-wedding plans.

'I don't want to diminish your enthusiasm,' Natalya offered with gentle affection. 'But we haven't discussed the when or where of it yet.'

'It's every mother's dream to help plan a daughter's wedding. The dress, the venue, flowers…all of it.' She caught hold of Natalya and whirled her around full circle.

'Okay,' Natalya protested with a light laugh. 'I totally get it. But let me talk to Alexei first.'

There was coffee, thick, black, aromatic to provide a finishing touch to the evening, and there was time to relax a little before her parents took their leave.

'Our time, I think,' Alexei decided as he drew Natalya into his arms. 'Ivana is in her element.'

She turned her face up to him, and trailed her fingers down his cheek. 'Prepare yourself for bridal magazines, material swatches…everything that goes towards a wedding. Which we need to discuss.'

He wanted to indulge her, run the shower, share it with her, and help ease the tense muscles formed from a long day. And he would, soon.

'How do you feel about a private family-only civil ceremony, a relaxed tropical island honeymoon, followed by a formal church wedding for family and friends?'

Natalya closed her eyes, then opened them again. 'Two weddings? Are you kidding me?'

'Think about it.'

'I'm endeavouring not to.'

'Your parents, a few close friends. No fanfare, followed by lunch, or dinner if you prefer…then we fly out for a week of rest and relaxation. A private island, no tourists. I know someone who owns the perfect place.'

It sounded appealing…becoming more appealing by the minute. 'And do it all over again in style…when?'

'Six, maybe eight weeks later.'

'I think that could be a plan.' She uttered a faint shriek as he lifted her into his arms and headed for the main bedroom, helped discard her clothes and his own, then he took her to bed.

It was bliss…utter bliss, as he massaged out the kinks in tight muscles, *more* as his hands shaped her body, lingered a little, then he took her to bed…to sleep curled close in against him.

Discretion was key in planning a private wedding.

Subterfuge a given.

What should have been simple in arranging a very private wedding ceremony took effort in a bid to avoid media attention.

The preferred setting narrowed down to two venues… The gardens at Ivana's home, or the grounds surrounding Alexei's home.

Alexei's Seaforth mansion proved the ideal choice, followed by a celebratory lunch prepared by Lisette.

'I'm calm,' Natalya assured Ivana as she put the finishing touches to her make-up.

Words, which didn't hold much weight, evidenced by the slight tremor in each hand as she tended to her hair.

There was a brief tap at the door as Lisette entered carrying a tray. 'I thought tea might be a welcome distraction.'

'How kind,' Ivana assured her with a smile. 'Will you join us?'

A small window of light relief helped ease the increase of nervous tension…which was crazy.

She loved Alexei with every cell in her body, every beat of her heart. *Sure*…as every breath she took, that his love for her was absolute.

Ivana offered a faint smile in silent understanding, almost as if she knew the train of her daughter's thoughts, and Natalya returned the smile, sipped the tea, then she discarded the silk wrap-around, and selected the white fine linen mid-calf dress overlain with guipure lace, elbow-length sleeves and a wide scooped neckline, stepped into it, stood still as Ivana slid home the long zip, before stepping back to offer a smiling nod of approval.

White stilettos, a wispy white confection of a cocktail hat, completed the outfit, Ivana handed her a bouquet of white roses culled from her own garden…and it became time to join Alexei waiting in the formal downstairs lounge.

Alexei cut a resplendent figure in a dark suit, white shirt and dark silk tie.

Ivana shared the role of matron of honour and mother of the bride. Roman gave the bride into Alexei's keeping, and Cristos, who'd flown in from New York, took the part of Alexei's best man.

A simple, heartfelt ceremony conducted by a celebrant…touching in that Alexei caught hold of her hand as she reached his side and lifted it to brush his mouth to her fingers, offered a deep emotive smile, then lowered his head to take her mouth with his in a soft lingering kiss.

It added to the informality, and brought a smile to those present.

The exchange of rings, hers a magnificent wide diamond-encrusted band, while Alexei had chosen a plain gold ring.

The kiss sealing their marriage was more evocative, loving, and tears shimmered in Natalya's eyes as she whispered, 'Love you.'

Lunch was a delight, with love, laughter…laidback and incredibly personal.

Lisette had excelled herself. Roman remained quiet, reflective, while Ivana appeared relaxed, delighted her daughter had found everlasting happiness with her first and only love.

Not journey's end, she perceived.

A beginning.

The choice of a tropical island paradise became their personal honeymoon destination.

Owned by one of Alexei's friends, it was off the tourist tracery of holiday island venues.

Small, unique, with live-in staff to cater to the smallest of any guest's whim. There was an indoor pool, private, with an electronic roof to let in the sun…if desired, or not. A lanai…with cushioned cane chairs overlooking an outdoor pool that appeared to meld into the sapphire blue ocean. A motorised yacht moored at the end of a long jetty.

Indoors a large central lounge, a home office, three large luxe bedroom suites each with an en suite bathroom. A games room, set up for billiards, table tennis. A sauna.

Together with a rich man's necessity…a heliport complete with helicopter.

Perfection, luxurious, a haven from the hi-tech world of international business. Yet everything on hand at the push of a button, if need be.

Staff quarters situated at one end of the island housed a married couple employed as caretakers, their eldest son who acted as chef when the owners or invited guests were in residence. A younger son who piloted the motorised yacht and helicopter, and a daughter who assisted with household chores.

It was divine, an experience to remember…infinitely special—as Natalya evinced at the end of their stay.

'We can always return,' Alexei assured as they boarded the helicopter for the return home.

It was the caretaker's youngest son who took the pilot's seat, and set the engine in motion.

'Something to look forward to,' Natalya said with a whimsical smile. Maybe in a few years, with a young child to laugh at puddles, make sandcastles, enjoy the sunshine unfettered by the rush and bustle of city life. Playschool, kindergarten…

It was good to be home, to complete the final move of her belongings to Alexei's mansion. To make decisions to lease her own apartment, interview prospective tenants…only to discover Ben had a friend who was looking for an apartment, possessed of impeccable references, solid employment, whom she had already met, knew, and without hesitation she offered a lease, stored her furniture, and was grateful for the done deal.

Work proved intense during their first week, with Alexei taking up the slack from their absence, involving long hours…evenings when it was almost midnight before they each hit the shower and fell into bed.

Only for life to settle back into a reasonably familiar routine…if you factored in a formal wedding to be held with Alexei's family as guests, close friends, ADE's office staff together with top personnel from ADE's industrial plant.

A wedding planner took care of the details, liaised and approved the caterers' menu…ensuring everything went as smoothly as possible.

Eight weeks after their intimate wedding, they enjoyed the best of the best…both families together, guests they'd requested to attend, a beautiful church favoured by Ivana's mother during her lifetime, and a stunning venue for the wedding breakfast.

The bridal gown surpassed Natalya's dreams, with an exquisite bodice of intricate lace moulded to showcase her upper body, a sweetheart neckline, three-quarter sleeves in lace, with layers of silk falling from the waist beneath pale ivory silk to boost the skirt's volume a little so the hemline touched the tips of ivory stilettos. A floaty veil completed the bridal gown, and only she and Alexei knew the slender gold chain at her neck held his original gift of the simple diamond ring nestling deep within the V between each breast. On her right hand she wore the magnificent solitaire diamond Alexei had gifted her, and which she'd worn as a betrothal ring at their private wedding.

Soon he'd place the wide diamond-encrusted wedding ring on her left hand, and they would formally be named husband and wife before a church filled with family and guests.

'Tilt your head a little. I need to blend the eyeshadow just a touch more.'

Natalya obeyed, and shot Anja a faintly wry smile. 'Tell me again why I agreed to do this?'

'Ivana,' Anja reminded her gently. 'Your mother is in her element. Her smile, the soft laughter, her bond with Alexei's mother and family is a beautiful thing to witness.

'Then there's Alexei, the gorgeous man you're already married to…'

'I get it. I really do.'

'So hush… It's a lovely day, the sun is shining, the wedding planners have achieved a magnificent setting. The photographers are due to arrive any minute. Each mother of the little flower girl and pageboy have everything in hand.' She tapped a light forefinger to the tip of Natalya's nose. 'Relax.'

She was tempted to roll her eyes, and refrained… barely. 'I am perfectly relaxed.'

'Uh-huh,' Anja responded, *sotto voce.* 'Perfectly.'

'Am I permitted to say I preferred my first wedding?' It had been so intimate, so laid-back. *Special.*

'Of course. But only to me.'

Her mouth curved into a genuine smile. 'Thanks for being here. For doing what you do best. Friend, the sister I never had. All of it.'

'You're welcome. And for the record…right back at you. What you said, and more.'

It became time to shed her wrap, and step into her wedding gown…exquisite, delicate, perfect.

'You look so beautiful,' Ivana complimented gently, almost on the point of tears.

Natalya caught her mother close. 'Please don't cry.'

'I'm so happy for you…both of you.'

A special moment, encapsulating the now, the promise of the future.

'I know,' Natalya said gently. And she did. 'Thank you for everything. All of it, for as long as I can remember.'

Her childhood, the happiness, laughter, and memories of three generations…the special times influenced by a different culture from a different country.

Ivana and Natalya drew apart, smiled, touched a hand to each other's cheek…and stepped out into the sunshine together where three limousines waited to transport the bride's parents in one, Anja with the two small children in the second, and the bride with Paul at the wheel ready to complete the procession.

This was the moment, Natalya reflected as the limousine travelled the suburbs en route to the beautiful old church her darling babushka had adored. Settled back from the road and accessed via a long curved driveway shadowed by trees, it captured a timeless era of tradition, faith and something more… almost indefinable. And familiarity, for all the occasions she had attended there with her grandmother and mother.

A year, even six months ago, she could never have envisaged she would be attending her own wedding. Or that Alexei would be waiting for her at the church.

A broken dream, never imagined to be realised.

Yet there were occasions when dreams shifted, reassembled and were resolved. As hers had been… by the hand of Fate.

Paul slowed the limousine to a crawl prior to making the final turn to the street where the church's entrance lay, and slowly travelled the gently curved tree-lined driveway, where a team of photographers captured the moment of the bride's parents' arrival, immediately followed by Anja and the two children… and minutes later by the bride.

Flashbulbs popped, almost blinding as they melded with the sunshine, and the media were there to record the scoop of the day that would feature in the evening's newspapers, and probably occupy a small segment on the TV news.

As a notable event, the wedding would attract attention…and better an organised compliant willingness to share, than have the gutter press issue their dubious take filched from supposition and unsubstantiated fact.

Consequently there had been a private interview with the press, vetted and approved prior to publication. Also a sanctioned photograph…both of which had been released prior to the wedding. Now it was time to seal their love sanctioned and blessed in the church of their choice.

Today would feature a touch of grandeur, of love, light and happiness…genuine, even to the most critical eye.

Nervous, much? A little, Natalya admitted as the limousine eased to a halt outside the main entry. She knew enough not to look directly at the flashbulbs, to smile, and appear composed.

To pause long enough for Ivana and Anja to straighten her veil, ensure the gown's hemline wasn't caught up, and surprise both women with an impromptu kiss to her mother's cheek, before bestowing a similar salutation on Anja.

'My only wish is for you to be happy,' Roman said quietly as they took the first steps down the aisle.

There was a time to put her father's transgressions in the past, to move forward with the future…and this appeared to be the appropriate moment.

Natalya turned her head to offer Roman a winsome smile. 'I am…very happy,' she assured him gently.

Then she took her father's arm, leant forward and said quietly, 'Let's do this.'

The aisle seemed long, and she took the first step, then another, looked up and saw Alexei ignored tradition and had turned to watch her progress.

Natalya simply focussed on his expression as she slowly closed the distance to his side, saw the way his mouth curved into a smile, the light, the love in his eyes…for her. Only her.

And her head lifted a little, her smile faintly teasing as they shared a silent promise mere words could not convey.

Perfect, so incredibly right as she drew to a pause at his side…totally unprepared as he lowered his head and bestowed a gentle lingering kiss, sensed her response, only to reluctantly withdraw and clasp her hand within his own as they both turned to face the beaming minister, oblivious to the light laughter of the guests.

Oh, my.

Natalya was conscious of the vows spoken, the solemnity of the service, the faint tightening of Alexei's hand as they were pronounced husband and wife.

The kiss was a mutual benediction, and they turned to face the guests, to the hand-clapping and the smiles as they slowly stepped forward, paused for Anja to set the flower girl and pageboy in their positions, then began the slow walk down the aisle…only to hear a child's startled cry, and turn to see Gigi had tripped and become momentarily disoriented, bent on ignoring Anja's soothing voice and helping hands… as the little girl turned and ran towards the closest person she recognised… Alexei.

Without hesitation he scooped her into his arms, soothed her tears, and touched his lips to her small forehead as she curled her arms round his neck.

Xena rushed from her seat, only for Gigi to shake her head and cling to Alexei.

'It's okay,' he offered gently as Xena looked distressed.

And it was. Gigi simply buried her head against Alexei's neck, and didn't lift it until they reached the vestibule where Cristos waited to extricate his daughter.

Natalya felt her heart melt at the sight of Alexei cradling his niece as if it was the most natural act in the world.

Aware he would do the same with their own children, be a hands-on father who would gift his heart, everything he had, to the well-being of his children… and for her.

There, whenever, wherever he was needed.

Because it mattered. As she mattered.

Evident in everything he did, the words said and those not needed to be voiced.

Love. Theirs alone.

Now, she waved aside Cristos's attempt at an apology. 'It was delightful,' she assured him with a genuine smile.

It became a talking point among the guests, who collectively accorded it a touching moment.

There were photographs, professional, the media,

family, video cameras recording the ceremony, before and after wedding snaps, laughter, smiles, the beautiful bonding between Calista and Ivana.

It was, in retrospect, a very special wedding. A blend of grandeur and contemporary...of love, family and friends who each came together to celebrate the joining of two people who had loved, lost, and found each other again.

The moment when Natalya and Alexei were alone, Alexei took hold of her hand and lifted it to his lips, then kissed the tip of each finger in turn.

It was the wedding waltz which almost brought her undone as she circled the floor in Alexei's arms. The lowering of his head as he brought his lips close to her ear and said, 'You're the love of my life. You... only you complete me.'

Uncaring of time or place, she reached up and touched gentle fingers to his cheek, caressed the groomed stubble, and rested fingers to the edge of his mouth.

'There are the words I could say,' she said quietly. 'And I will, because I need you to hear them. I want to touch you, to show you you're the other half of me. My love, soul-mate...my everything.'

He pulled her close against him, held her there... his arousal a potent force. 'Let's get out of here.'

It was easy to smile, to tease a little. 'It's our night. We get to choose.'

They finished the bridal waltz, circled the room with unhurried steps, pausing to thank their guests individually for attending the wedding celebration, spent a little time with each of their parents and family, then slipped away from the venue to a waiting limousine with Paul at the wheel. For he, too, had been a valued guest.

'Home?'

'Yes. Please,' Natalya added, as she nestled her head into the curve of Alexei's shoulder. Perhaps the best gift she could give him was the one she'd been waiting days for the right moment. When would be better than now?

There was more. Just a few words, and she offered them later...much later after they'd made love, tears gathering at the edge of her eyes as she relaxed in his arms.

'This morning I took a pregnancy test.'

She didn't make him wait.

'It was positive.'

EPILOGUE

LIFE WAS GOOD, Natalya reflected as she carefully eased the sated babe from her breast. The night was still at this pre-dawn hour.

'There we go, my little darling,' she murmured with a loving smile as she hugged Nikos close and brushed soft lips to his forehead.

This was their time, so precious and special, and she quietly began singing a soft lullaby of a small babe falling asleep in a cradle as she gently rocked him in her arms, smiling at the sound of his customary burp.

She wanted to hold him a little longer, to stroke light fingers over his soft cheek, and to give quiet blessings for the miracle of life. And she did, silently, with all the love in her heart.

Then she carefully placed him into his crib, reached out and lowered the baby night lamp, paused to double-check he was sleeping, then she turned to leave the nursery…and saw Alexei's tall frame leaning against the door frame.

'How long have you been standing there?' Natalya

queried quietly as she drew close, and in the dim light she caught his slow smile.

'A while.' He lifted a hand and curved it beneath her chin. 'I like to watch you both together.' He pressed his thumb-pad to her lips. 'Share the bond between mother and child.'

A lump rose in her throat, and she swallowed it down. 'You're a great father.'

A wonderful support during the initial few months of her pregnancy, when he took time out to accompany her to every appointment—there at her side through every injection, each examination. Marvelling at each sonogram as they watched their son develop in the womb. Counting fingers and toes, the moment when it appeared the unborn babe turned and appeared to look at them.

Choosing a name, agreeing on his late grandfather's name... Nikos.

Alexei touched his mouth to hers, gently at first, then he curved an arm around her shoulders.

He was a good babe, suckled well, only woke once through the night for a feed, then slept until the early pre-dawn hours. He tended to smile...although Natalya felt sure it was simply wind.

Natalya cast Alexei a musing glance. 'This is one of the best times of the night. The day is done, Nikos is sleeping, and...'

'It's our time,' he assured her quietly and pulled her into his arms and deepened the kiss before raising his head to touch his lips to her temple. 'I love you.'

Her eyes filled, and she blinked to hold back the tears. How could she not know?

'You touch a hand to my cheek, and my heart begins to dissolve,' she said gently.

'You're the other half of me.' His lips traced her own, nibbled a little, then soothed. 'I sense every move you make during the night, and draw you close.'

She held back the threat of tears. 'Returned in kind. Every word. All of it.'

How could she not, when he'd read everything available on pre-natal care, gowned in the operating theatre during the caesarean section?

His was the first face she saw after the birth. The gentle kiss he bestowed as she offered him a wondrous smile as she was given their son to hold for the first time.

Now, she reached up to cradle her husband's face. 'Let's go to bed.'

His smile almost undid her. *Love*…all of it, and more, clearly evident. For her.

'You need a few hours' sleep before Nikos will want his next feed.'

'Uh-huh.' Natalya pulled his head down to hers. 'And I'll have them.'

A touch, the light drift of fingers over sensitised skin.

All consuming, captivating as the senses coalesced in the joining of mind, body and soul.

The completion of the circle of love. Sensual magic.

'But first,' she teased gently, 'I want to make love with the main man in my life.'

Alexei smiled in the dim moonlight filtering through the shuttered windows. 'I have no problem with that, *agape mou*.'

* * * * *

If you enjoyed
ALEXEI'S PASSIONATE REVENGE,
why not explore these other
Helen Bianchin stories?

ALESSANDRO'S PRIZE
PUBLIC MARRIAGE, PRIVATE SECRETS
THE ANDREOU MARRIAGE ARRANGEMENT

Available now!

COMING NEXT MONTH FROM
♦HARLEQUIN
Presents®

Available January 16, 2018

#3593 THE SECRET VALTINOS BABY
Vows for Billionaires
by Lynne Graham
Merry Armstrong couldn't resist Angel Valtinos's sensual charisma—he awakened her with his touch and left her pregnant! Valtinos's legacy *must* be legitimised, but seducing Merry into marriage will be his biggest challenge...

#3594 A BRIDE AT HIS BIDDING
by Michelle Smart
Undercover journalist Carrie Rivers is playing a dangerous game with Andreas Samaras. When her ruse is revealed, there's only one way to protect Andreas's reputation: blackmail Carrie to the altar!

#3595 CLAIMING HIS NINE-MONTH CONSEQUENCE
One Night With Consequences
by Jennie Lucas
It's not what he wanted, but Ares Kourakis is going to be a father. He'll dutifully marry Ruby, but will intense passion and a vast fortune be enough to get her down the aisle?

#3596 BOUGHT WITH THE ITALIAN'S RING
Conveniently Wed!
by Tara Pammi
Pia Vito is heir to CEO Raphael Mastrantino's billion-dollar empire—so he initiates a calculated seduction! But when inescapable longing engulfs them, to make her his, Raphael must give her more than a diamond ring!

#3597 THE GREEK'S ULTIMATE CONQUEST
by Kim Lawrence
Grief-struck Nik Latsis found oblivion with a stunning stranger. Since then, Chloe's haunted his dreams. Only another taste will rid him of his desire, but first Nik must entice feisty Chloe back into his bed...

#3598 A PROPOSAL TO SECURE HIS VENGEANCE
by Kate Walker
Imogen O'Sullivan is horrified when Raoul breaks up her engagement and makes her his own convenient bride—he's planning a passionate punishment for their stormy past! Can Imogen resist Raoul's delicious revenge?

#3599 REDEMPTION OF A RUTHLESS BILLIONAIRE
by Lucy Ellis
Nik Voronov is ferociously protective of his grandfather. When he believes Sybella Parminter is taking advantage, he strips her of her job! But unexpected desire soon threatens to consume them both...

#3600 SHOCK HEIR FOR THE CROWN PRINCE
Claimed by a King
by Kelly Hunter
Prince Casimir never forgot his wild nights of abandon with Anastasia Douglas. Years later, he discovers she had his daughter! And he'll stop at nothing to claim them both...

Get 2 Free Books,
Plus 2 Free Gifts—
just for trying the
Reader Service!

She succumbed to his sinful seduction…
Now she's carrying the Greek's baby!

It's the last thing he wanted, but Greek billionaire
Ares Kourakis is going to be a father. He'll do his duty
and keep pregnant Ruby by his side—he'll even marry
her. But will his offer of intense passion and a vast
fortune be enough to get idealistic Ruby down the aisle?

Read on for a sneak preview of
Jennie Lucas's next story,
CLAIMING HIS NINE-MONTH CONSEQUENCE

One Night With Consequences

Ruby.

Pregnant.

Impossible. She couldn't be. They'd used protection.

He could still remember how he'd felt when he'd kissed
her. When he'd heard her soft sigh of surrender. How she'd
shuddered, crying out with pleasure in his arms. How he'd
done the same.

And she'd been a virgin. He'd never been anyone's first
lover. Ares had lost his virginity at eighteen, a relatively
late age compared to his friends, but growing up as he had,
he'd idealistically wanted to wait for love. And he had, until

he'd fallen for a sexy French girl the summer after boarding school. It wasn't until summer ended that his father had gleefully revealed that Melice had actually been a prostitute, bought and paid for all the time. *I did it for your own good, boy. All that weak-minded yearning over love was getting on my nerves. Now you know what all women are after— money. You're welcome.*

Ares's bodyguard closed the car door behind him with a bang, causing him to jump.

"Sir? Are you there?"

Turning his attention back to his assistant on the phone, Ares said grimly, "Give me her phone number."

Two minutes later, as his driver pulled the sedan smoothly down the street, merging into Paris's evening traffic, Ares listened to the phone ring and ring. Why didn't Ruby answer?

When he'd left Star Valley, he'd thought he could forget her.

Instead, he'd endured four and a half months of painful celibacy, since his traitorous body didn't want any other woman. He couldn't forget the soft curves of Ruby's body, her sweet mouth like sin. She hadn't wanted his money. She'd been insulted by his offer. She'd told him never to call her again.

And now…

She was pregnant. With his baby.

He sat up straight as the phone was finally answered. "Hello?"

Don't miss
CLAIMING HIS NINE-MONTH CONSEQUENCE,
available February 2018 wherever
Harlequin Presents® books and ebooks are sold.

www.Harlequin.com

HARLEQUIN *Presents*®

Next month, look out for Kelly Hunter's Harlequin Presents debut! Her sinful Claimed by a King quartet stars four powerful rulers, dedicated to duty—until they meet the only women to threaten their iron resolve! In *Shock Heir for the Crown Prince*, Anastasia kept their child a secret. Now Casimir will make her his royal queen…

Prince Casimir of Byzenmaach can't shake the memory of Anastasia Douglas. With her, he forgot his royal duties in a moment of wild abandon. Seven years later, he must wed—but in seeking out the unforgettable Anastasia, he discovers a secret: she gave birth to his daughter! And he'll stop at nothing to claim them both…

Shock Heir for the Crown Prince
Available February 2018!

King Theodosius must find a queen—so he offers Princess Moriana an initiation in the pleasures of the marriage bed…

Convenient Bride for the King
Available March 2018!

And look for Augustus of Arun's and Valentine of Thallasia's stories
Coming soon!